"Hi, all," the guy said with an English accent.

As Jack introduced the group, Joey, Jen, and Sarah all eyed Trevor with interest. As far as Jen was concerned, any girl breathing would do the same. Trevor was six feet tall, muscular, and tanned, with short, spiky black hair and eyes the same blue as the lake. He wore a red T-shirt that read "Manchester United," and soccer shorts.

"Call me psychic, but I'm guessing you're English and that, by the looks of your legs, you work out on a regular basis," Jen said flirtatiously.

"That's brilliant. Give the gorgeous blond girl a Kewpie doll," Trevor said, laughing. His eyes slid over to Joey. "Didn't catch what Joey is short for, love."

"That would be 'cuz I didn't throw it," Joey replied.

He smiled, revealing twin dimples. "I'm guessing Josephine."

"You're guessing right," she admitted.

He nodded. "Suits you. And—it's Sarah, right?"

"Right, Alas, no nickname," Sarah sighed. "What would people call me, Sar?"

"You've got great definition, love," Trevor told her. "You weight train?"

"I've been known to," Sarah acknowledged.

"Great, we can hit the weight room together sometime," Trevor said. His sexy grin took in Jen, Joey, and Sarah. "This is going to be one helluva summer, ladies. Don't you think?"

Dawson's Creek™

Playing for Keeps

Based on the television series "Dawson's Creek"™
created by **Kevin Williamson**

Written by C. J. Anders

First published 2000 by Pocket Books a division of
Simon & Schuster Inc., 1230 Avenue of the Americas,
New York, NY 10020

This edition published 2000 by Channel 4 Books
an imprint of Macmillan Publishers Ltd
25 Eccleston Place, London SW1W 9NF
Basingstoke and Oxford

www.macmillan.com

Associated companies throughout the world

ISBN 0 7522 7224 1

This book is a work of fiction. Names, characters, places and
incidents are products of the author's imagination or are used
fictitiously. Any resemblance to actual events or locales or
persons, living or dead, is entirely coincidental.

9 8 7 6 5 4 3 2 1

A CIP catalogue record for this book is available from
the British Library.

Printed by Mackays of Chatham PLC, Chatham, Kent

For Bears everywhere

Chapter 1

"It's finally summer!" Dawson Leery exclaimed, throwing his arms wide. "No more teachers, no more books, and other trite but true sayings along those lines."

"The day of our annual Saturday-afternoon-after-school-ends-for-the-year 'Free at Last' picnic," Joey Potter proclaimed, "wherein we stuff our faces and contemplate how to spend our misspent youth."

"Yo, Dawson, be useful and help me with this blanket," his best friend, Pacey Witter asked. The two guys grabbed both ends and let the old beach blanket float down onto the lush park grass. All around them, families and couples who had the same idea for a picnic had spread out as well. The delicious aromas of barbecue wafted by on the summer breeze.

"I think that mustard stain is from last year's picnic." Jen Lindley pointed to a yellow-orange ring on the blanket.

"Which would follow, since this blanket has been in the back of my father's truck since last year. Think of it as the polyester equivalent of fine wine, aging and improving, as it molders in the flatbed," Pacey suggested, lifting his face to the hot afternoon sun. A fishing boat motored by out in the channel. "I ask you, is there anything better in life than the first day of summer vacation? All those in agreement, signify by saying 'Yeah, baby!' "

"Yeah, baby!" his friends dutifully echoed, plopping down on the blanket next to Pacey. Joey immediately began to unpack a large, ratty-looking picnic basket.

"Please keep in mind as you dig into my cold roast chicken," she warned, "that I am well aware that cooking is not my long suit."

"Admittedly we were all physically ill after last year's delightful ptomaine-laced egg salad," Pacey commented ruefully, "however, we lived to tell the tale, and that's what counts, Potter."

She gave him an arch look. "And just what did you contribute to this moveable feast?" He lifted up his boom box, then punched in the numbers for the Boston oldies rock station.

"Pacey, this is not a *Big Chill* moment," Jen told him. "Do you think you could track down a radio station that offers tunes from, say, this millennium?"

"Here's your million-dollar question, Jen," Pacey said as he played with the equalizer on his boom box. "What is the name of the tune currently being played? Is it (a) a boring alt song, (b) a plagiarized rap so-called song, (c) a been-there-crooned-that country song, or (d) the one and only Motown mojo, Mr. Marvin Gaye, singing 'Sexual Healing'?"

"Be glad he's not forcing 'Disco Inferno' on us," Dawson said as he pulled plastic forks and spoons out of a paper bag he'd brought along. "Here, everyone." He tossed plastic utensils to his friends.

"He tries it and we stuff him into a Nehru straitjacket," Jen said threateningly.

"Trust me, eating this chicken is punishment enough," Pacey mumbled through a mouthful of drumstick. "It gives new meaning to the term 'overcooked,' Chef Potter."

"So I left it in the oven a little too long," Joey admitted. "I was baby-sitting Alexander and he had a temper tantrum and spit up on the floor. I guess time just got away from me."

"For what, days?" Pacey grabbed his soda and guzzled it to try to wash down the dried-out chicken.

"Ignore him," Jen advised Joey. "He's a cretin who can't appreciate good cooking."

"As always," Joey agreed. She spooned some homemade potato salad onto her paper plate. "Can you believe we're going to be seniors next year? It just seems so . . . so final."

"Joey, we've been out of school for less than twenty-four hours," Jen said. "What say we save senior-anxiety obsession for at least another day or two."

"You're right," Joey agreed. "I tell myself that all

the time. It's just that myself is notorious for not listening. Pacey, can you turn that down?"

Dawson swallowed a large bite of Joey's dried-out chicken as Pacey reluctantly turned the volume down on his boom box. "I suggest we worry in a more linear and immediate fashion. For example, last I heard, despite this nation's supposedly booming economy, none of us had yet secured summer employment."

"Last I heard, at least one of us wasn't looking," Pacey pointed out. He lay on his back, his hands under his head. "I plan to spend long summer days and hot summer nights on major cruise control, doing things I will greatly regret once I mature."

"You told me that you were going to work at Mack's Shack," Joey reminded him. "Selling overpriced junk food to hungry tourists on the Capeside beach and smiling ingratiatingly at them in pursuit of large tips. You told me that you need to start saving money for college."

Pacey lowered his sunglasses so he could see her better. "Ya know, Potter, you have this tendency to put a damper on things. I'd watch that if I was you."

"All I meant was—"

"Joey, Joey, Joey, you're talking while Marvin sings, an act that is a capital felony in many states," Pacey said. He jumped to his feet, then pulled Joey up with him. "You can't not dance to Marvin."

Joey rolled her eyes and was about to sit down again when Jen stood and started dancing with Pacey, kicking off her shoes in the lush grass. For some reason, as awkward as it made Joey feel, she couldn't let Jen do what she wasn't willing to do. So she got up and started moving too.

Dawson watched the three of them, a faint smile on his face. They had all come so far this year. He and Joey had gone from couple mode to best-friend mode—which didn't necessarily mean they couldn't slip back into couple mode again. You just never knew. Joey was still the person he felt closest to in the world. Nothing could ever change that.

Dawson watched as Jen danced with her hands over her head, doing some kind of sexy thing that looked perfectly natural for her. It seemed so long ago that Jen had moved in next door with her grandmother, but it had only been only two years. One day, there she was, this golden girl from New York. Gorgeous, sophisticated, sexy, smart. And nice. He'd fallen for her, hard and fast.

Funny. Because after Jen, he and Joey were—no, that was too tough to think about on such a beautiful day. Now, he was just "friends" with both Joey and Jen. And yet sometimes his feelings for Joey were . . .

Complicated, Dawson thought to himself. *Very complicated.*

"This is how life should be," Pacey said, dancing comically in a circle around Jen and then Joey. "Two gorgeous women for every guy. I've changed my mind. If there are any summer jobs with this description advertised in the paper, I might go for an interview."

The song ended and the threesome plopped back down on the blanket. Jen drank down half her soda.

"Seriously, Pacey, are you going to work with Mack this summer?"

"Frankly, it sounds deadly," Pacey replied, leaning back on his elbows. "He's been running that junk-food shack on the beach every single summer of my life. The man must excrete essence of French fry by now. He wants me to be the fry cook. It must be a thousand degrees in his kitchen."

"Sounds stultifying," Jen agreed.

"Actually, I think being stuck indoors renting videos all summer sounds worse," Dawson mused.

Jen clapped her hands against her cheeks in *Home Alone*-style surprise. "What? Dawson Leery, boy film genius, doesn't want to spend the summer among his cherished filmic ancestors and friends?"

"I was thinking of something that did not require the restocking of kid vids as a life skill," Dawson said.

"I need to find a job too," Jen admitted. "Oh, for the grand old days when I had free use of Daddy's dear American Express card."

Joey dug her hand into the bag of chips and extracted a handful. "Well, Potter's B&B is not exactly packing 'em in. If I could find some kind of part-time thing, and still be there to help Bessie, that would be perfect."

Pacey shook his head. "People, what happened to being young, hormonally driven, and irresponsible? What happened to young slacker attitude of the twentieth century?" he asked them. "I am deeply disappointed in you."

Jen leaned back and watched a few fleecy clouds

6

floating by. "Remember when you were a little kid and summer vacation seemed to go on forever and ever?"

"I used to have this fantasy, every summer, that I could reinvent myself," Joey recalled. "I'd come back to school in the fall and be someone completely different. Someone who wasn't 'Joey Potter from the wrong side of the tracks.' I'd think about that all summer long. Obsess, really."

"Come on, Jo, we used to have a blast in the summer," Dawson said. "I don't remember you obsessing."

Joey looped her hair behind her ear. "What, you presume that's something I'd actually *tell* you?"

"Yes, actually."

"Well, sorry Dawson, but you presumed wrong. Not that you and I weren't as close as the *Sweet Valley* twins and all, but I thought you had this perfect life so I wasn't about to admit my stupid little fantasy to you."

Dawson smiled wryly. Joey was right, in a limited way. There had been a time when he thought his life was, if not perfect, then close to it. But then his parents had separated, which had been the shock of his life. Then they got divorced. And those were only the beginning of the changes that he knew had rocked his world.

Jen rolled over onto her stomach and propped her chin up with her fist. "Is it just me or are we a tad too self-involved, here?"

"Many tads," Pacey commented. He tossed a tiny marshmallow into the air and caught it in his open mouth. "Hey, Potter, didn't you tell me that Andie and Jack were coming to meet us here?"

Joey nodded. "That's what Andie told me. She's bringing the desserts."

"Well no offense," Pacey said, "but the girl can bake, and as your fossilized chicken was not exactly finger-lickin' good, I'm being reduced to eating puffy white squares of pure sugar before your very eyes."

"Keep in mind that next year it'll be your turn to make the food," Joey reminded him. "I have committed every slight to my culinary skills to memory. And I'm very big on payback."

"Next year will be graduation, and I'll simply bribe McPhee to cook for me," Pacey decided.

"With what?" Jen asked, laughing. "You don't have anything she wants."

"Why not ask her that?" Joey suggested brightly, cocking her head toward Andie and her brother, Jack. They were heading toward them, loaded down with bags and baskets. "There are few things I enjoy more than listening to a woman tell you off, Pacey."

"The McPhees arrive bearing gifts," Jack announced. He dropped two beach bags and an overstuffed picnic basket next to the blanket. Andie carefully placed another, equally overloaded-looking basket next to the first one.

"I hesitate to ask what could possibly be in all that stuff," Jen said. "Dessert for two hundred? And locker room supplies for the Patriots?"

"Close. The beach bags contain every item Andie could think of that might be used for post-dining entertainment," Jack explained. "You've got your

Frisbees, your softballs, and your badminton set, your footballs for the requisite game of two-hand touch, not to mention various levels of sunblock."

Andie began to systematically unpack one of the picnic baskets. "And since I knew it was Joey's turn to do most of the cooking this year, I thought culinary reinforcements would be appreciated. Chicken salad with walnuts, grapes, and chutney; white albacore tuna salad with a hint of dilled mayo; homemade sourdough bread; and tomato-basil focaccia."

"You're a goddess, McPhee," Pacey said, pulling off a hunk of sourdough bread.

"And in here," Andie began, opening the other picnic basket, "we have china, silverware, and cloth napkins. I thought it would make things more elegant."

Joey threw her hands into the air. "I throw myself on my sword and accept defeat. Speaking of, toss my so-called chicken to the terns." She took a chicken wing and hurled it toward the waterside, where three or four white birds did noisy battle over it.

Dawson eagerly filled a plate with the food Andie had brought. No doubt about it, she was a diehard perfectionist, and this spread seemed excessive even for her. It had seemed to Dawson that when Pacey and Andie had been a couple, she'd mellowed out somewhat. But, of course, they weren't a couple anymore.

"This is delicious," Jen told Andie.

"There are times when your unwillingness to be second best is a blessing," Joey agreed, as she savored Andie's chicken salad. "If only we could afford to hire you to cook for Potter's maybe we'd have actual customers."

"Oh, you guys, speaking of summer jobs," Andie said, putting her plate down. She licked some tuna salad off her finger, then reached into one of the beach bags. "Did any of you read the want ads in today's newspaper?"

"Can't say that I did," Jen replied as Andie unfolded the classifieds section of the newspaper. Everyone else's mouth was still full.

"Listen to this." Andie read an ad to them. "Camp Takabec, located on beautiful Capeside Bay just outside of Capeside, seeks summer staff. Camp Takabec is a sleep-away camp for boys and girls ages seven through fourteen. Positions available include general counselors as well as specialists in various sports, performing arts, and academic tutoring."

She looked up at her friends. "And it says that interviews are tomorrow, Sunday, from nine to noon, right at the camp," she continued. "Doesn't this sound fabulous?"

"Camp Takabec. Isn't that the camp that all the rich kids from Boston used to go to?" Joey asked. "I thought it was called something else."

"Camp Homeric," Pacey filled in. "It got sold last winter. My brother was actually talking with some of the other cops about buying it." He shuddered. "Can you imagine Deputy Doug running a summer camp for kids?"

"That's right. I think I heard something about it being under new management," Dawson recalled. He scratched his chin thoughtfully. "Actually, working at a summer camp isn't the worst notion in the world."

"But it's close to it," Pacey pointed out. "Might I remind everyone that a summer camp for rich kids is full of pampered and screaming brats whom the staff must treat like rare porcelain, because the parents of the aforementioned brats can afford to pay over-priced summer camp bills because they are all senior partners at gigantic law firms?"

Jack cocked an eye at him. "Isn't that a little heavy on the reverse snobbery?"

"Only if it weren't true," Pacey replied.

"You guys, come on," Andie cajoled them. "What if we all got summer jobs at Camp Takabec? It would be a blast."

Joey scraped the last of the chicken salad off her plate and licked it off her fork. "It's not an option for me. I need a day job so that I can be home to help Bessie with the bed and breakfast at night and cook breakfast the next day. That is, if we ever have any customers."

"Well, maybe there are day jobs," Andie said. "You could ask, at least."

"I suppose I could," Joey reluctantly agreed.

Pacey drank down the last of his soda. "I have to admit, the idea of employment that allows me to sleep in accommodations that do not also accommo-date Sheriff Witter and his eldest offspring has a cer-tain allure. After all, a guy needs his space."

"I was thinking along those lines, myself," Jack said. "In my case, I could definitely deal with a change of scenery."

"Okay, so we're all in on this, right? Good. How

about if I call and set up interviews?" Andie pulled her cell phone out of one of the beach bags.

"Your prep work boggles the mind," Jen said.

"Thank you," Andie said serenely. She began to punch the number given in the advertisement into her cell phone. "And by the way, I'm taking your silence as a unanimous 'yes.' "

Chapter 2

"Hey, everyone. I'm Mike Takermann."

Lanky, handsome Mike looked to be in his mid-thirties. He wore a baseball cap, shorts, and a gray Camp Takabec T-shirt. At the moment he was standing on the stage of the Takabec Playhouse, flashing his newly hired camp staff a group-disarming smile.

"I don't trust that grin," Pacey told Joey, leaning close so that no one else would hear.

"Give the guy a chance," she whispered back.

Pacey, Joey, Dawson, Jack, Jen, and Andie were all sitting together, midway from the front, in a playhouse full of people who looked to range from age sixteen to age sixty. It was the day before camp would start, which, according to the handout they'd all been given when they'd been hired, made it Camp Takabec Staff Orientation Day.

"I'm the new owner of Camp Takabec," Mike continued. "I want to welcome you all to orientation. I think we have a killer staff—give yourselves a round of applause!" Mike began to clap and most of the assembled staff joined in. Joey noticed a girl in the next row with a red ponytail who was clapping so enthusiastically she looked like she was about to fall off her seat.

Joey dubiously joined in the applause, as did her friends. Jen looked over at Joey and raised her eyebrows.

"Now, that's the Camp Takabec spirit, you guys, way to go!" Mike told them. "As most of you know, Camp Takabec had a long and esteemed tradition as Camp Homeric before I purchased it over the winter; I definitely plan to uphold that tradition and to build upon it."

As Mr. Takermann continued on about the proud tradition of the camp, Joey's mind began to wander. It was hard for her to believe that all six of them had been hired so easily, but that's exactly what had happened. Her interview had been a snap, and the others had told her theirs had been equally easy. In fact, their interviews had been one right after the other.

Joey had been called into Mr. Takermann's office first. "Call me Mr. Tack," he'd told Joey heartily, and invited her to have a seat. He'd made a quick perusal of her application, then leaned forward and said, "Let me ask you this, Joey, bottom line. Do you like kids? 'Cuz camp is about kids."

She'd answered in the affirmative, he'd asked her about her interest and experience in art, and, twenty-four hours later, she'd gotten a phone call from a secretary telling her she was Camp Takabec's arts and crafts specialist. Mr. Tack had readily agreed that she could commute to the job rather than sleep at camp. The job paid $110 per week. Counselors who had specialties as well as being responsible for a group sleeping in a bunk were getting $150 a week.

The whole thing seemed almost too good to be true. It had been so easy for all of them to get hired that Joey could only surmise that Mr. Tack had been experiencing something of an employment crunch. Fortunately, it had worked in her and her friends' favor.

Dawson had been hired as something called the film arts director, which evidently meant helping kids to make their own videos; Jack was coaching football and general sports; Andie was an academic tutor; and Jen and Pacey had talked their way into being co-heads of the drama department.

"Some of you are camp pros and others of you are new to this," Mr. Tack was now saying to his staff. "At the risk of stating the obvious, all staff will eat all meals in the camp dining hall with the campers except on your every-other-week day off. Those of you who are counselors in charge of bunks will get the full camping experience. Generally speaking, each 'bunk' is run by two counselors. Some bunks are small log cabins; others are giant canvas tents, complete with eight army-issue cots and a cold-water bathroom. But that's what makes camp so great!"

"They charge rich kids a fortune to live like they're

in a third-world country?" Joey whispered to Dawson. "And doesn't this guy ever stop talking?"

He shrugged and smiled at her. She couldn't help but smile back. He had the exact same smile he'd had when he was a little boy. Though she was careful not to let him know it too often, it still melted her heart.

"Any questions?" Mr. Tack asked the assembled group. The girl with the red ponytail shot her hand into the air.

"Yes—remind me of your name again, please. I can't read your name tag from here," Mr. Tack told her.

"Georgia Garvey, but everyone calls me Gigi, I'm your girls' cheerleading specialist," she announced. "I'm a little concerned about the cold showers thing, because that can lower the immune system. Also, I'm a total vegan who is allergic to dairy, so I'm a little concerned about the camp food also, thank you."

Joey had to hand it to Mr. Tack, his grin didn't slip. "We provide very nutritious meals, and hot water is available for showers at one site on each quad in the showerhouse. I don't think you'll have any problems, Gigi."

"Super!" She sat back down.

"Allrighty," Mr. Tack said, rubbing his hands together with anticipation. "Let's get you assigned to your bunks and then go for a group walk around the camp grounds—I'll give you the grand tour. Then we'll return here to the playhouse at eleven to continue our orientation. Bunk assignments are posted on the bulletin board right outside the playhouse. Be sure to pick up your camp uniforms too—they'll be charged against your account. Move 'em on out!"

Mr. Tack jumped athletically off the stage and jogged to the rear of the playhouse as the staff rose to follow his lead. But most of the counselors held their places, grumbling with discontent. "He didn't say anything about a camp uniform in our interview," Andie groused. "I believe that is called a sin of omission."

"We have to pay to be fashion-challenged?" Jen asked. "There's something deeply wrong with that."

"Hey, we all want to get off on the right foot, I'm sure," Mr. Tack called. He'd heard the grumbling and wanted to calm his staff. He climbed back up on the stage. "Is there a problem here? Does someone have something to say?"

Gigi's hand headed north instantly and Mr. Tack fixed her with a none-too-happy gaze. "Yes, Gigi?"

"I'd like to know why you're only telling us now about having to wear camp uniforms, and why you're charging them against our salaries. It isn't fair to drop this on us now. I was planning to wear my cheerleading outfits from home to inspire my girls."

"Where's home, the state of Rah-Rah?" Jen muttered to Jack, who was sitting next to her.

"Good point, Gigi," Mr. Tack said. "Let me explain the Camp Takabec philosophy to you. Camp uniforms are a great equalizer. And while it is true that Camp Takabec is an expensive proposition for many parents, it is also true that I offer scholarships to many deserving young campers. Now, we don't want those young campers of lower socioeconomic back-

17

grounds to feel singled out in any way, do we?" Gigi shook her head, and her ponytail swished back and forth.

"That's why all campers wear uniforms. Now, your uniforms reverse the colors on the T-shirt, so that campers are different from counselors. But would we want our campers to see some counselors dressing rich and others dressing poor, Gigi? Is that the message we want to send here at Camp Takabec?"

"I definitely see your point," Gigi said.

"Excellent, Gigi." Mr. Tack smiled at her again. "We'll all wear uniforms at all times on camp grounds. They're pretty darn keen looking and will be yours to keep when the season is over."

Andie leaned close to Joey. "I don't know about you, but I have a feeling mine will live in a dark drawer when the summer ends." Joey nodded her agreement.

"Okay, super!" Mr. Tack exclaimed. "Let's see that Camp Takabec spirit, guys! Jog on out there and find your bunk assignments and we'll take the grand tour in fifteen minutes."

"Lucky me, no bunk assignment," Joey reminded her friends.

"Maybe it'll be fun," Jen mused. "Of course, I have no basis for comparison. I was a let's-go-to-Europe-for-the-summer kid, not a summer-camp kid."

"Well, I was a summer-camp kid," Andie said. "And so was Jack. I loved it."

"And I hated it," Jack put in. "Which is why I'm so looking forward to lording it over these poor kids."

Andie hit his arm playfully. "You are such a bad

liar. You'll be the sweetest counselor in the world."
She turned to Jen. "Come on, let's go find out where
we ended up."

The girls went outside, while Dawson, Pacey, and
Jack waited inside for the crowd to thin out. "What
do you think, Pace?" Dawson asked.

"I think that compared to our wilderness experience in the wilds of *Deliverance* country, and the
charming drill sergeants who busted our chops that
first day, this is your basic piece o' cake. I say we
make a pact. Under no circumstances will we allow
Mr. Tack to ruin our summer."

"I'm in," Jack agreed, grinning, as he sidled up to
the two of them.

"That makes all three of us," Dawson said, and
they fist-bumped all around to seal the deal.

As they headed out the door, Pacey added, "The
first thing we do is figure out how we get out of camp
at night after the wee ones are asleep. This camp
counselor thing might just work out after all."

Jen found her name and bunk assignment on the
bulletin board, then worked her way through the
crowd and back over to Joey and Andie. "I'm leading
the Nightingales," she told them. "Seven girls, age
thirteen. And my co-counselor is someone named
Charma Billie."

"No one is named Charma Billie," Joey said.
"That's like a made-up name."

Jen shrugged. "I'm assuming the bulletin board
doesn't lie." She glanced around. "I wonder who
she is."

"She's me."

Joey and Andie turned around, where a deep voice had growled. But rather than the Amazon they were expecting, they saw a very petite woman with a scowling face who looked to be in her forties. She had long brown hair shot with gray that she wore in a tight braid down her back. She already had on a Camp Takabec outfit, which was pretty amazing, Jen thought, because the outfits hadn't been handed out yet, as far as she knew.

"The full name is Charma Belinda Pennysworth," the woman said to the two of them. "And don't call me Charming, because I'm not. You are—?"

"Jen Lindley," Jen replied, sticking out her hand to shake Charma's. "And these are my friends, Joey Potter and Andie McPhee. We live in Capeside."

Charma nodded tersely. "Let's get the shock factor out of the way, shall we? I'm forty-eight years old. I'm a schoolteacher in Boston during the academic year, and I've been working as a counselor at Camp Homeric for thirty consecutive summers. My good sense told me not to return when Homer Thiessen sold the camp, but at this point I think it must be programmed in my genes to be here in July and August."

"That's very interesting," Andie began, but clearly Charma wasn't finished, because she went right on.

"Yes, my father is Chilton Pennysworth III, the famous theater critic, and, no, I didn't agree with his glowing review of the Helen Keller musical *Helen!* that everyone got so all fired up about. I thought the show was pure garbage and I told him so. I'm not married, no kids, and I'm the head of the waterfront. Does that answer your questions?"

"Likely, if I'd had a chance to formulate them," Jen replied dryly.

"What bunks did you girls draw?" Charma asked. If she was offended by Jen's light gibe, she didn't show it.

"My family has a bed and breakfast in Capeside, so I'm commuting," Joey explained, "but when I'm not running arts and crafts, I'm supposed to help out with the Robins, fourteen-year-old girls."

"I have the Finches," Andie said. "There's no other counselor listed, and, according to the bulletin board, there's no co-counselor. I wonder what that's about." Charma laughed uproariously.

"So glad I amuse," Andie told her. "Hopefully, we'll be laughing, too, when you let us in on the joke."

"Did you by any chance list 'baby-sitting' as job experience on your application?" Charma queried.

"Yes," Andie said. "So?"

"First rule of camp applications: Never, ever, *ever* write 'baby-sitting' down on an application. Finches are the new girls, age seven, who have never been away from home before. More often than not, camp freaks 'em out because they're really too young for sleep-away camp. They bring plastic sheeting with them, if you catch my drift." Andie stared at her blankly.

"Potty accidents on a regular basis," Charma explained, still chuckling. "Your life is about to become a sopped-in-the-morning living hell. I had seven-year-olds my first summer at camp. Never again."

Andie sighed. "Well, at least I only have four of them. How bad can it be?"

Jen and Joey looked at her. "Bad," they both said.

Charma shook her head. "I'm telling you, girls, camping isn't what it used to be. Why, back when Camp Homeric was in its heyday this place was overrun with children. Absolutely overrun! They had manners and discipline too. But now, parents want to send their kids on preteen tours to Egypt, or they're divorced and don't see their children during the year and are so overwhelmed with guilt that in the summer, they take their kids on lavish vacations with a nanny, of course, and—"

A shrill blast from the whistle that hung on a lanyard around Mr. Tack's neck cut her off. Thankfully.

"Gather 'round, people!" he called, waving to them. "It's tour time."

"I know this joint better than he does," Charma said. "Catch you young ladies later." She took off toward the waterfront at a brisk pace.

"Why do I think that she and I will not be sneaking out together at night to go meet cute boys?" Jen pondered.

"She probably eats cute boys for breakfast, lunch, and dinner," Andie said.

"It's kind of terrific, though, that she's been doing this for so long," Joey mused. "I mean, she must really love kids, don't you think?"

Jen rolled her eyes. "Ten bucks says they don't love her back."

"Come on, people, time's a-wasting!" Mr. Tack called out, then blasted his whistle again.

A tall girl with long auburn hair approached Joey. She wore a blue tank-top shirt and jeans, was large-boned and athletically built. She looked something like Picabo Street, the Olympic skier.

"Excuse me. Some guys over there told me you're Joey Potter?"

"Yes, that's me."

"I'm Sarah Gulliver," the girl said, holding out her hand to shake Joey's. "We're going to be counselors of the Robins together."

"Nice to meet you," Joey said, returning Sarah's smile. She liked the girl on sight.

"I heard that you worked a deal so that you don't have to sleep in the bunk," Sarah said. "Tack told me one of the nurses is bunking in with us instead. How'd you manage that?"

"I think Mr. Tack was desperate."

Sarah laughed. "All I'm asking is that you invite me over to your house as often as possible."

Joey laughed. "I'll see what I can do. We do run a B&B. Although let me warn you that my sister, Bess, puts all nonpaying visitors on bathroom-cleaning duty. It's her way of discouraging freebies."

"After a couple of weeks with the kiddies, even that might sound attractive," Sarah said. "Anyway, I cleverly purchased and packed an inflatable woman who, according to the label, is named Caress. I plan to leave Caress to snooze in my place until I get back to camp after midnight curfew."

Andie laughed. "That's funny! Can you imagine anyone actually—" She realized Sarah wasn't laughing. "Wait. You mean that wasn't a joke?"

"Only time will tell," Sarah replied mysteriously.

Mr. Tack's whistle cut through the morning sunshine again. "Okay, people, listen up!" he called, cupping his hands by his mouth for volume. "Just follow me, I'll lead you through camp. There are signs posted in front of everything so that I won't have to shout. Let's go get 'em!"

Andie dutifully trotted after him, leaving the others to lag behind.

"There is something just a little too gung-ho about this man," Jen opined, as she, Joey, and Sarah set off in the pack trailing behind Mr. Tack.

Dawson waited until they caught up with him. "Hey, how's it going?"

Sarah eyed Dawson with obvious interest, so Joey made quick introductions.

"And how many little darlings are you in charge of?" Jen asked him.

"That would be me and Pacey," Dawson told her. "We're co-counselors to a group of fifth graders, the Bears. For some demented reason, I'm actually starting to look forward to it. How about you?"

Jen told him about her encounter with Charma. "I mean, you have to ask yourself why a woman that age would be a camp counselor, unless she basically had no life."

"This way, people!" Mr. Tack led the group across a large baseball field, then past three tennis courts, a basketball court, some paddle tennis courts, and onto a quad of bunks. Here he stopped.

"This is where the boys have their bunks. All ages, from seven through fourteen. On the other side of camp is the girls' area, same arrangement. I count on my counselors to help maintain decorum. Archery, riflery, soccer fields, etcetera, off to my left. More tennis courts and ballfields to my right. Also the areas for film, camp newspaper, radio and electronics, etcetera."

Joey raised her hand. "How about arts and crafts?" she asked.

Mr. Tack smiled. "Good question. "We've relocated down by the bay side, along the main lodge, waterfront facilities, and dining halls. Let's go down there now." He glanced at his watch. "Double time." He started jogging across the boys' quad, following the incline toward the bay front.

Joey turned to Jen. "Call me crazy, but does this place not bear a suspicious similarity to the camp where our wilderness adventure took place?"

Jen shrugged. "Maybe there's one guy out there who is the world expert on camp design, and he lays 'em all out the same way."

"As long as the activities aren't the same," Joey said, shuddering. "Those early morning runs were killer."

They reached the bay front. There was indeed, just as at Wilderness Camp, a large dining hall built out over the water. Hard by the dining hall was the swimming area—there were dozens of sailboats moored out beyond that. The staff milled around on the beach, while Mr. Tack got into an administrative huddle with his office assistants.

"Hey, guys," Pacey said, strolling over to them. "How cool is this place? I'm picturing a Bill Murray

Meatballs–era kinda thing. He got the cute girl, right?"

Pacey's eyes lit on Sarah. "Speaking of which . . ." He stuck his hand out. "Hi. Pacey Witter."

She shook it firmly. "Sarah Gulliver. Nice to meet you."

Pacey grinned. "Right back atcha."

"Friends, Romans, fellow camp slaves," Jack called as he headed toward them with another guy in tow. "How goes it?"

"It goes," Joey replied.

"I want you guys to meet Trevor Braithwaite," Jack said, nodding at the guy standing next to him. "He's my co-counselor for soccer."

"Hi, all," the guy said with an English accent.

As Jack introduced the group, Joey, Jen, and Sarah all eyed Trevor with interest. As far as Jen was concerned, any girl breathing would do the same. Trevor was six feet tall, muscular, and tanned, with short, spiky black hair and eyes the same blue as the lake. He wore a red T-shirt that read Manchester United, and soccer shorts.

"Call me psychic, but I'm guessing you're English and that, by the looks of your legs, you work out on a regular basis," Jen said flirtatiously.

"That's brilliant! Give the gorgeous blond girl a Kewpie doll," Trevor said, laughing. His eyes slid over to Joey. "Didn't catch what Joey is short for, love."

"That would be 'cuz I didn't throw it," Joey replied.

He smiled, revealing twin dimples. "I'm guessing Josephine."

"You're guessing right," she admitted.

He nodded. "Suits you. And—it's Sarah, right?"

"Right. Alas, no nickname." Sarah sighed. "What would people call me, Sar?"

"You've got great definition, love," Trevor told her. "You weight train?"

"I've been known to," Sarah acknowledged.

"Great, we can hit the weight room together sometime," Trevor said. His sexy grin took in Jen, Joey, and Sarah. "This is going to be one helluva summer, ladies. Don't you think?"

Chapter 3

"**B**ears' camper bios, Bears' camper bios, get 'em while they're hot!" Pete Takermann called out as he approached Dawson and Pacey's bunk. Pete was eighteen, a gangly freshman at the University of New Hampshire, with a protruding Adam's apple and an unfortunate skin condition. He was also both Mr. Tack's number-one assistant and nephew.

It was the next morning. Following a staff breakfast of cereal, cold burned toast, and scrambled eggs the consistency of papier-mâché, all the counselors had been told to report to their bunks, unpack their campers' trunks and make their beds, and await the delivery of camper bios. Camper bios, Mr. Tack had explained, were dossiers on each of the kids that would be in their care for the summer.

"This way you'll have a jump start on each kid's

likes, dislikes, strengths, weaknesses, and so on,"
Mr. Tack had said. "I have to tell you people, I'm
darn proud of the work Pete and his assistants put
into compiling this for you. Let's give it up for Pete!"
The staff had dutifully applauded.

So now, the trunks unpacked and the campers'
beds all made, Pacey and Dawson had been waiting
outside the Bears bunks, seated on two sawed-off
tree stumps, for at least an hour, waiting for Pete's
arrival.

"Hand 'em over," Pacey said. Pete dropped a stack
of file folders into Pacey's hands.

"Campers start arriving right after lunch," Pete
reminded them. "My uncle wants you guys to com-
mit to memory what's in those bios before the kids
get here. It's critical."

"We're memorizing even as you speak," Dawson
assured him.

"Great. Catch you later." Pete gave them a salute
and tramped off toward the next bunk.

"How much can there possibly be to say about
ten-year-olds?" Dawson pondered as Pacey handed
him half of the stack of folders. Each folder had a
kid's name on top. Next to that, a small photo of the
camper had been paper-clipped.

"Smelkowitz, Melvin," Dawson read off the top
folder. "Melvin Smelkowitz? How would you like to
be ten and stuck with that name?" The kid in the
photo had brown hair and eyes and looked like a zil-
lion other kids, even if his parents had given him a
really awful bad name.

Dawson opened the folder and read:

Melvin, age ten, is an academically advanced student entering fifth grade at a private school in Boston in the fall. He excels in reading and math. His best sport is pocket billiards. His parents are the owners of Smelkowitz Flowers, a national floral service specializing in arrangements for special arrangements.

"Amazing. This kid is the son of the 'Make time to stop and Smelkowitz the flowers' guy," Dawson told Pacey. "The one who does those annoying TV commercials."

"Great. Maybe we'll get daily arrangements delivered to the bunk," Pacey mumbled, his head buried in another file.

Dawson read on.

Melvin has had some social interaction problems in the past. He may need support in the area of personal hygiene. At his school, he's been given the nickname Smelly, which only exacerbates the problem. We discourage all campers from name-calling or using derogatory nicknames, and Melvin has been the butt of such humor in the past

"That's nothing, Dawson," Pacey said, looking at the folder in his hands. "Listen to this one."

Walter Carrier, age ten, is a great all-around kid entering fifth grade in a New Haven, Connecticut, public school. His father is a doctor and his mother is a paralegal. Walter is very chunky. As a defense mechanism, he sometimes uses it to intimidate others. This behavior is to be discouraged. Walter is not fond of athletics but his parents would like him to be encouraged to participate in them this summer. His interests include singing and writing rap songs.

Pacey held up Walter's photo. "Blond as a Viking. And roughly the size of a Sumo wrestler."

Dawson winced. "What are we, the Bears Bunk for Seriously Dysfunctional Kids?"

They quickly went through the rest of their files—

Kenny Reebeck:	dealing with some hostility issues.
Alan Berman:	has had a problem with stealing but his parents report that this is now under control.
Caesar Fleming:	an excellent athlete with germ phobia.
Andrew Casparian:	albino computer genius; has permission to bring his laptop to camp.
Jason Phillips:	loves athletics, great all-around kid.

When they'd reached the end of the last file, Pacey and Dawson stared at each other, until Pacey burst out laughing. "This has to be a practical joke," he sputtered.

"I beg to differ. Mr. Tack doesn't look like a man with a highly developed sense of humor," Dawson replied. "And that also applies for his dermatologically challenged nephew."

Pacey dropped the file folders onto the stump where they'd been sitting. "It's like they put every loser kid in our bunk, with the exception of—what's his name—Jason Phillips."

"Keep in mind that you might have been referred to as a loser kid when you were ten," Dawson reminded Pacey.

"Exactly my point! I am one-hundred percent positive that the parentals of these borderline cases would not want their children under my influence."

"Come on, Pace," Dawson implored his friend. "You'll be great with kids who have a few problems. What about Buzz? You've already proven you're good with kids. They'll probably all hero-worship you."

"Somehow, when I think of being the object of hero worship, scantily clad, loose-moraled college sophomores come to mind," Pacey mused.

Dawson laughed, then picked up the files. "Dream on. Let's bring these inside before our campers arrive."

"I can honestly say that was the worst hamburger I have ever eaten," Jen declared as she eyed the remains of it on her lunch plate.

"I'm not sure that beef was graded for human consumption," Dawson agreed.

"Well, Joey's cooking notwithstanding, we all know I have no culinary standards," Pacey said.

"And we don't know what they'll be serving tonight when the campers arrive. Which is why I downed two of those bad boys."

He patted his well-satiated stomach as Joey looked around the dining hall, which was a sea of gray and green. Everyone wore their official uniforms: the gray T-shirt with "Camp Takabec" lettering and gray shorts with "Camp Takabec" embroidered on the pocket. Dozens of conversations were in progress, the counselors realizing that this was going to be their last meal for a while without the accompaniment of their campers.

Jack and Andie were sitting with Trevor two tables over, and Joey saw Trevor chatting with that annoying cheerleader chick, Gigi. In the brief time she'd been able to see Gigi in action, she reminded Joey way too much of a camp version of Belinda McGovern, head of the Capeside High cheerleaders. That is, thoroughly cute on the outside, thoroughly rotten on the inside. Exactly the kind of girl who would revel in throwing Joey's scandalous background—dad in prison, no money to buy the "in" little outfits from whatever was the current "in" little boutique—back in her face. Or, to share it with whomever might care to listen.

Not that I actually know Gigi is like Belinda, Joey thought. *I haven't even spoken to the girl. But sometimes you just get a feeling about someone.*

"You thinking about Mr. Hottie over there?" Jen teased, cocking her head toward Trevor.

"Definitely not," Joey said. "Clearly he thinks enough of himself already."

Jen watched Trevor and Gigi for a moment as Trevor made Gigi laugh. Then, Gigi grabbed his muscular biceps and squeezed.

"You know who Gigi reminds me of?" Jen asked.

"Belinda McGovern," Jen and Joey declared at the same time.

"You too, huh?" Jen folded her arms. "Definitely not a good omen," her words punctuated by a shrill whistle from Mr. Tack, who stood up at the head table.

"I have already developed a deep antipathy to that thing," Dawson said, wincing at the sound of the whistle.

"Okay, people, our campers will start arriving in the next fifteen minutes," Mr. Tack told them. The acoustics were good enough in the dining hall that his voice easily carried. "I hope you're all as excited as I am. Everyone should have on his or her name tag. Remember the drill: We meet and greet as kids arrive and register; we walk the camper to the appropriate bunk, then we head back for more. Everyone should have arrived by four o'clock, at which point we'll assemble with our campers for our first bunk meetings. Any questions?"

Gigi's hand shot into the air. "Figures," Joey muttered.

"Yes, Gigi?"

"I just wanted to say, Mr. Tack, on behalf of your new staff, that we plan to make this the most fantastic summer ever." She beamed at the camp director, and he beamed right back at her.

"That's neat, Gigi. Way to go with the attitude,"

Mr. Tack told her. "You've got that Takabec spirit. Okay, staff, let's go get 'em!"

"That Takabec spirit?" Joey echoed as they all pushed out of their chairs. "I am so not a camp spirit, rah-rah kind of girl."

"And I did my short penance in cheerleading hell, thank you very much," Jen reminded her.

Pacey draped an arm around Dawson's shoulders as they headed out into the afternoon sun. "Let's go greet our seven dwarves. They may be geeky misfits, but they'll be our geeky misfits."

By the time all the counselors walked up the hill toward the camp arch, parents' cars and even some chartered buses had begun to pull into the parking lots. Within a half-hour, the camp was a madhouse, with kids screaming, crying, laughing, fighting, and whatever else they could think of to do while their counselors got them organized.

Andie dutifully stood by the door of a bus that had just pulled up, waiting for the kids to disembark. "Hi, I'm Andie, welcome to Camp Takabec," she repeated over and over as kids began to step down. "Go right over there to register. Hi, I'm Andie, welcome to Camp Takabec!"

"Nice knockers," a freckle-faced boy who didn't look more than ten years old told her as he swaggered off the bus. "We'll have to hook up later."

Andie watched in a state of shock as the kid with the freckles headed over to the registration. The nerve! Nearby, Charma was chatting with a mother who held a little girl's hand. The girl had blond pigtails, and tears streamed down her cheeks.

"I want to go home!" she begged her mother.

"But you told me you wanted to come to camp just like your big sister, remember?" the mom said.

"I don't care, I'd rather go home." She looked up at Charma. "I hate you."

"She doesn't mean it," the mother said quickly. "She's just scared."

"No problem," Charma said cheerfully. "I'm sure she's a sweet child and she'll get along just great here. Let me introduce her to her counselor. Andie?"

Andie, who had heard the entire conversation, walked over to them. "Hi there," she told the little girl. "My name is Andie McPhee. What's yours?"

"You're annoying," the little girl declared, then buried her head in her mother's stomach.

"I'll just leave you two to bond," Charma told Andie, strolling off to greet some other campers.

"I'm so sorry, Andie. Lillith never acts out like this," the mother told Andie.

"Maybe she really isn't ready for overnight camp," Andie suggested. "She's seven?"

"Seven and a half. But she begged. And it's all paid for, no refunds. Her big sister, Athena, is here. I'm sure she'll be fine. My husband and I are leaving for Europe tomorrow."

"Right," Andie said, nodding.

"Lillith, why don't you let Andie show you your cabin? She's going to be your bunk counselor."

Lillith peeked out at Andie. "Can I use my Barbie sheets on my bed?"

"Sure," Andie said, although she had no idea whether or not Barbie sheets were allowed. Lillith finally kissed her mother goodbye and held Andie's hand as they headed for their bunk.

"So, tell me, Lillith," Andie asked, "did your mommy happen to pack any little plastic sheets to go under your Barbie sheets?"

"Two sets," Lillith replied. "So you can take turns if you have to."

Swell.

Joey surveyed the seven ninth-graders in her bunk. They were fourteen, the oldest kids permitted in camp. They were all sitting on their beds, affecting some measure of cool as she and Sarah Gulliver ran them through orientation. But it seemed like all of them were repeat campers from Camp Homeric, and they knew the camp better than either she or Sarah did.

"So, Sarah and I are here for you guys, you can always come to us," Joey told them.

"Sure, whatever," the tallest girl said.

Joey cringed inside. She'd immediately been concerned when she'd found out that they were in charge of girls who weren't much younger than themselves, but actually the campers seemed to appreciate it, so that wasn't the problem. The problem was that the girls were already developing a pecking order that was bound to make some of them miserable all summer. And they hadn't been in their bunk for more than a couple of hours.

"Hey, Joey, do you know what the camp play is going to be?" a girl named Tia Bixley asked. She had straight brown hair held back by an out-of-style headband and a too-serious face.

"No, I don't," Joey replied. "Do you, Sarah?"

"Not a clue."

"But my friends Jen and Pacey are in charge of it,"
Joey told the girl. "So I'll find out for you, how's that?"

Tia nodded. "I was Joan of Arc in our school production of *Joan of Arc.*"

"Gag me," the tall girl muttered. Joey recalled now
that her name was Britney Sloan. Britney had
straight blond hair and looked like she was eighteen.
The other girls in the bunk already seemed to be in
awe of her, and they tittered at her comment. Tia
blushed with embarassment.

"Listen you guys," Sarah said, "it's really important
that we all stick together as a bunk."

"You mean like we're a sorority?" a girl named
Kendall asked. She had already established herself
as Britney's friend and had taken the bed next to
Britney's.

"Sure, if that works for you," Sarah replied.

"Oh, it works fine for me," Kendall said. "Except
that when you're in a sorority, you get to choose who
you pledge."

"Well, that's not the Camp Takabec spirit," Joey
told her. "Exclusion is not going to cut it here."

Britney and Kendall traded looks. "One other
thing," Britney said, eyeing Joey. "If you're not sleep-
ing in the bunk, who's the other nighttime counselor
besides Sarah? Because it's in the camp contract
with our parents that we have two counselors. Not
that we need any."

"I was told that one of the camp nurses would
bunk with you guys," Joey explained.

"Oh, that's great," Kendall groaned. "They usually bring them in from the army."

Joey looked at Sarah, who shrugged helplessly. This was not a good beginning. Clearly Britney and Kendall were used to being the popular ones, dictating who was in and who was out.

And clearly they had already decided that Tia was out.

"I've got an idea. How about if we go around the cabin and you can all tell one another a little about yourselves?" Sarah suggested. It was on Mr. Tack's get-to-know-each-other to-do list, so she didn't have much of a choice.

"Do we have to?" Kendall whined. "That is, like, so weenie. Most of us know each other from past years here, and it doesn't look like anyone's changed much. Right, Tia? You look exactly the same, in fact." Tia didn't respond.

"How about if people who want to speak do, and people who don't can just say 'pass' when we get to them?" Sarah asked. "I'd like to try this."

"Pass in advance," Britney sneered.

"Pass," Kendall added.

"Pass!" Tia cried, a bit too loud, trying to do the cool thing. Britney and Kendall looked sideways at her and then at each other. Then the two of them cracked up. All the other girls started laughing too.

Sarah stood up. "Okay, listen. We need to talk about a girl-power attitude in this place. Dissing other girls in the bunk is not—"

Her words were cut off as the bunk door swung open. There in the doorway stood Gigi, her red ponytail tied with gray and green ribbons to match her uniform.

"Hey! I'm Gigi!" she cried, as if she was about to launch into a cheer.

"May I help you?" Joey asked stiffly.

"Sorry I'm late," Gigi apologized. "I'm the night-time counselor for your bunk and I wanted to stop in and introduce myself."

Joey got a sinking feeling in the pit of her stomach. "I thought some nurse was going to—"

"Change of plans," Gigi sang out. She threw her arms open wide. "Girls, you've got me!"

Chapter 4

"Good evening, fair lady," Trevor called to Joey, jogging a few steps to catch up with her. It was after eight that evening, and they were both heading down to the beach.

"Hi." Joey's eyes slid over to him. He was definitely much too cute for his own good. Or hers, for that matter.

"On your way to the bonfire?" he asked pleasantly.

"Since it's required of the entire staff to be at the opening-night bonfire, what do you think?"

Trevor winced. "Have I said or done something that rubbed you the wrong way? Do I look like an old boyfriend who broke your heart?"

"Hardly," Joey replied.

"So, you're just this rude to everyone who tries to

make pleasant conversation by the light of a glorious full moon, then?"

"It wasn't my intention to be rude and I'm sorry if I came off that way," Joey admitted. "I just . . . I have a lot on my mind."

Trevor gave a mock bow. "Apology accepted."

They walked along in silence for a moment or two. "Do you know that in the moonlight your hair has the loveliest red glints in it?" he asked.

Joey stopped walking and turned to him. "Look, Trevor, let's get something straight right off the bat. I'm quite sure glib flirtation is extremely successful for you, and I wish you all the luck in the world with whatever females at this camp happen to bleep on your I'd-love-a-piece-of-that radar, but I'm not going to be one of them."

He threw his head back and laughed. "Josephine, you're priceless!"

"It's Joey, and I'm also serious," Joey told him. "Excuse me, I need to catch up with my campers and they're already down at the bonfire." She took off at a trot, leaving a bemused Trevor behind.

She stopped when the beach came into view, spread out below the dirt road. A huge bonfire was burning on the beach. All campers ten and older were there, as well as all the counselors and staff who weren't minding the younger kids. Their bodies were silhouetted against the firelight and the moon glinted off the calm bay water.

A group of girls off to one side had already started some sort of camp song. She couldn't make out the words, but it was being sung with great enthusiasm.

She'd never gone away to camp as a kid. Not enough money. Plus her mom had been sick for so long that Joey would have refused to leave her even if there had been money.

I wonder what it would have been like, she thought now. The camaraderie, the feeling like you were a part of it all, that you belonged . . .

"Joey," Dawson said softly, coming up next to her.

"Hi." She smiled at him.

He cocked his head toward the beach. "It's fun down there. My bunk just put away about five boxes of toasted marshmallows."

"I was just thinking the same thing. Is Pacey there with your kids now?"

Dawson nodded. "I had to go back for Andrew's asthma inhaler. He's fine, but he panics if he doesn't have it on him at all times." Dawson held it up. "How about you?"

"Sarah took our kids down a little while ago. I had to drop the camper dossier files off at administration so that we wouldn't risk having our little darlings read what the powers that be have written about them. I forgot to bring them back earlier."

Dawson nodded solemnly. "Sounds like a potentially life-warping possibility."

Joey folded her arms. Now she could distinctly hear Kendall and Britney's voices in the singing. "These girls in my bunk . . . I'm only two years older than they are, but compared to them I feel like I should be slugging back Geritol and Ensure Plus and dropping my teeth in a glass. Were we that young at fourteen?"

"Probably. We better head down to the beach."

They began to walk toward the beach together. Joey filled Dawson in on the unwelcome addition of Gigi as the third co-counselor in her bunk. "Do you and Pacey have good kids?"

It took Dawson a moment to answer. " 'Good' might not be exactly the correct adjective."

"Interesting? Smart? Funny? All of the above?"

"Let's put it this way," Dawson said. "Pacey and I will be spending the summer running our own junior version of *Revenge of the Nerds*."

"Hey, hi!" Gigi cried, running over to them as soon as they reached the beach. "Super, Joey, you're just in time to help the girls toast marshmallows. Someone told me that they're made with horse hooves like Jell-O, but I checked on the Internet before I got to camp and found out some brands don't use gelatin." She turned to Dawson. "Hi! I'm Gigi!"

"Dawson Leery." They shook hands.

"Want to roast marshmallows with us, Dawson?" Gigi asked. "I'll hold your stick." She batted her eyelashes coquettishly at him.

"I think Dawson is quite capable of holding his own stick, Gigi," Joey snapped.

"Most boys start doing that around sixth grade," Dawson added, trying to keep a straight face. "I was a late bloomer, though."

Gigi giggled. "You're very cute, Dawson. Well, catch you later." She grabbed Joey's hand and dragged her off to their assembled bunk of girls. Pacey made his way through the sand to Dawson.

"Thank God you're here, I am in serious need of backup," he said. "Did you get the kid's inhaler?"

Dawson held it up. "What's going on?"

"Let's just get back to the Bears before they eat each other alive," Pacey suggested.

The Bears were hanging together on the side of the bonfire closest to the lake. Dawson handed Andrew his inhaler and the kid immediately took a few hits off of it.

"Ah. Much better."

"But you weren't having an athsma attack!" Pacey exclaimed.

"That wheezing thing you did this afternoon is nasty, man," Walter Carrier told him. "You be all choking and like that. What's up with that, dude?"

"Asthma is a disease that involves the bronchia," Andrew began. "Air passageways become clogged and swollen with phlegm—"

"Never say that word!" Caesar Fleming yelled, his right hand flapping spasmodically in the air.

"What word?" Andrew asked. "Asthma?"

"The F word!" Caesar shrieked.

"Who said the F word?" Melvin asked eagerly. "That's my favorite word!"

"Not that F word, turd breath," Caesar said. "I meant 'flem.'"

"The word 'phlegm' begins with a *p*," Andrew stated. "The correct spelling is—"

"No one cares, freak!" Walter boomed, belly-bumping the small boy with his massive bulk. "Hey, how come you be so white, man? You glow."

"I have a lack of pigmentation," Andrew replied calmly. "And why do you talk like you're an urban gangbanger when you live in the suburbs?"

45

"What, you never heard Eminem?" Walter challenged. "He's white and he be getting down with the homies, making beaucoup bucks and getting all the primo babes, you know what I'm sayin'?"

Andrew stared at him. "Frankly, no."

Walter belly-bumped him again. "What's it to you anyway, Casparian?"

"Hey, dudes," Melvin piped up, "Casparian's so white we oughtta call him Casper for short." The Bears cracked up, pointing at Andrew and laughing. Andrew calmly took another hit off of his inhaler.

"These kids are relentlessly cruel to each other," Dawson whispered to Pacey. "This is terrible."

"And it's only the first day of camp," Pacey pointed out. "Plus, that's only the beginning of the fun and games of our Bears. The Smelkowitz kid over there hasn't brushed his teeth since preschool. It's dangerous getting downwind of him. Alan Berman—he's the kid over there mooning those girls—"

"I remember their names, Pacey. Don't you think we should stop him?"

"That's one option. He's our little kleptomaniac in residence. Watch out for your stuff, and don't bring anything valuable into the bunk that you can't do without. He already stole Walter's candy stash and Melvin's *Playboy* magazine."

"*Playboy*?" Dawson echoed. "They're ten!"

Pacey shrugged. "Ten ain't what it used to be, my friend."

"Well, clearly, we need to intervene." Dawson started toward the boys, but Pacey stopped him.

46

"Hold up there a minute, partner. Let's think this through. Do we really want to spend the entire summer playing big, bad adult to these guys? Thankfully, I am not exactly role model material. I've had enough of that crap done to me. I'm sure as hell not doing it to some other kid."

Dawson hesitated, not sure what to do. He turned to watch the kids, considering his options. Most of them were pointing at Andrew and jeering "Casper!" Melvin was running around going "Ooh" in a fake, ghostly fashion.

Andrew calmly walked over to Melvin. "Excuse me, Mr. Smelkowitz. Can I have a moment of your time?"

"Yeah, Casper?"

"Did we or did we not attend the same summer camp last summer?"

"Yeah. So?"

"So someone else gave me the nickname Casper way back then, last year, Mr. Smelkowitz. I suggest you not take credit for another's insults. And might I add that since your personal hygiene clearly hasn't improved since last summer, I might as well tell our bunkmates your nickname. Melvin Smelkowitz, better known as Smelly."

"You do kinda reek, man," Kenny Reebeck agreed. He'd edged over to listen.

"Casper right. Your teeth be green, dude," Walter added. "Nasty."

"Dawson, Pacey, just the men I was looking for!" Mr. Tack called, heading across the sand with his arm around a kid they didn't know.

Pacey waved. "I bet that's our missing Bear," he told Dawson.

"Jason Phillips," Dawson recalled. "The only kid in our bunk whose bio lacked potentially sociopathic behavior."

"And he's a nice-looking kid," Pacey noted. "Maybe he'll become the Bears' ringleader and they'll all kinda rise to his level."

"Hey, how's it going?" Mr. Tack asked, clapping Dawson too hard on the back. "As you know, you guys were one Bear short at check-in this afternoon. This little rascal just got here. Better late than never. This is Jason Phillips. We're excited to have him at camp this summer. Jason, these two great guys are your counselors, Dawson and Pacey."

"Welcome to camp, Jason," Pacey told him, holding out his hand for Jason to shake.

"Alrighty, then," Mr. Tack said, nodding. "Ghost stories start soon, men. Big fun!" He saluted them and headed off.

"So, did you get your stuff to the Bears' bunk okay?" Dawson asked the kid.

He nodded, smiling.

"Great. Come on, Jason, I'll introduce you around."

Melvin was rushing up to the other kids, opening his mouth and breathing heavily on them, while they ran from him in mock terror.

"Smelly, get outta my face, man!" Walter yelled, waving the air in front of his face.

"His breath pales in comparison to his flatulence problem," Andrew reported calmly. "Wait. You'll see."

48

"Nah, you'll *smell!*" Smelly grinned proudly, bending over so that his butt faced Caesar, who flailed around like a fish on the beach.

"Hey, guys, I want you to meet Jason Phillips," Dawson told them. "He's the missing member of our bunk."

" 'Zup?" Walter asked, offering a meaty fist for a fist bump.

Jason just smiled and nodded.

"Why're you so late?" Alan Berman asked suspiciously.

Jason nodded and smiled again.

Pacey and Dawson exchanged looks. Something was clearly amiss. But what? This was supposed to be their one shot at a normal kid.

"We're just about to roast some marshmallows," Pacey told the kid. "You interested?"

Jason nodded again.

"Hey, don't you talk?" Caesar asked.

"I talk, yes," Jason replied in an accent so thick his words were barely discernable. Of course, this cracked the Bears up.

"Where you from, Mars?" Smelly asked. " 'Cause you sound like it."

"New Jersey," Jason replied. It came out as New Cher-sce.

"Nuh-uh," Kenny said. "I have cousins in New Jersey and they have a way different accent."

"Before I am Slovakia," Jason explained.

"Say *what?*" Walter asked.

"I think he means he's from Slovakia," Dawson explained. "It's in central Europe. It used to be Czechoslovakia, but . . ."

Jason nodded. "I am here two week only wid . . . how do you say . . . sister of my mother."

"Aunt," Pacey filled in. He and Dawson exchanged looks. Nothing in Jason's bio had mentioned that the kid wasn't American. And if he was from Slovakia, how did his name become Jason Phillips?

"Whatever," Walter said, nodding vigorously. "I think you cool, man."

"You cool," Jason agreed.

"Come on, man. We got us some weenies to roast. You in?"

"I like to roast my weenie, yes," Jason agreed.

"Roast this!" Alan yelled, thrusting his hips out and pointing at his crotch. Dawson watched in dismay. He felt a hand slip around his arm. It was Jen.

"These your little guys?" Jen asked. The Bears were now running, jumping, and pointing at their crotches as if it was the world's funniest joke.

"Much to my horror, yes," Dawson admitted.

Jen smiled. "They're cute."

"They're malicious farm animals, actually," Pacey said cheerfully. "How's it going, Jen?"

"Well, my co-counselor, Charma, is, as promised, not charming. But my girls seem cool. Thirteen is such a rough age."

"I believe that was the year I went into hormonal overdrive," Pacey recalled.

Jen smiled. "Too bad I wasn't in Capeside to help you steer."

"Hey, she your girlfriend?" Alan asked, looking Jen up and down.

"She's my friend," Dawson corrected. "Jen Lindley."

Alan wriggled his eyebrows. "Hubba-hubba! How good a friend?"

"Hey, mates!" Trevor called, padding over to them, Frisbee in hand. "Anyone up for some disc action? It's glow-in-the-dark so you can see 'er coming. Jen?"

"No thanks. I have to get back to my girls."

"I think they can probably do without you for a few," Trevor coaxed.

"I'm sure they can, but I'm not really in a night-Frisbee mood," Jen explained.

"Hey, he wants to get into your pants!" Alan bellowed, cracking up all the other Bears.

"Cheeky kid," Trevor said, chuckling. Then he leaned close enough to Jen so that the kids couldn't hear. "He's right, of course."

Jen regarded Trevor, a bemused look on her face as she considered the possibility. "Interesting," she mused. "Very interesting."

"Also rather presumptuous," Dawson added.

Trevor looked at Jen. "He your father figure?"

"More like bodyguard."

"Dawson! Dawson!" Gigi rushed over to him. "Hi! Oh, hi to the rest of you too." She grabbed Dawson's hand and swung it as she spoke. "Mr. T says it's time for ghost stories, and Joey says you knew the greatest ghost story about some place called Witch Island and you even made a movie about it, so could you tell it, pretty please?"

Dawson managed to extricate his hand from hers.

"Well, it's really better told through the medium of film, so—"

"But Joey says it's so scary and there really is a Witch Island near here. Come on, the kids would love it, they all wished they could see *Blair Witch* but it was rated R. Please, can you?"

"Please, Dawson?" Jen added teasingly. "For the kids who couldn't sneak into *Blair Witch* or whose parents wouldn't rent it for them to shut them up?"

"I suppose I can reconstruct the basic log line," Dawson agreed.

"Fantastic!" Gigi threw her arms around him and kissed him. The Bears went insane at this, whistling, hooting, and making lip-smacking noises.

"Hey!" Alan yelled to Gigi, pointing at Dawson. "He wants to get in your pants!"

Gigi put her hands on her hips and gave Alan a chastising look. "Now, is that a respectful way to talk to me?"

Alan blushed red and shrugged.

"No it is not, Mister. Now, where's my apology?"

"Sorry," Alan mumbled, staring at the sand.

"That's better. Dawson does not want to get into my pants. I think that's settled." She leaned close to Dawson, her breasts pressing against his biceps.

"However," she whispered in his ear, "I do want to get into his."

Chapter 5

Pacey was having the greatest dream—starring himself, twins who looked a lot like Cameron Diaz, and a stick shift—when the bugle blast exploded in his brain. It was reveille, courtesy of Pete Takermann's silver bugle, amplified over the Camp Takabec sound system.

Three days into the job, three reveilles, each compliments of Pete. Pacey snapped awake, then pulled his pillow over his head, mentally telling Pete just what he could do with his bugle. "Let's go, let's go, let's go, up and at 'em!" Mr. Tack was walking around the quad, literally banging on bunk doors with a canoe paddle. "It's a gorgeous Capeside morning, time's a-wastin'. Let's up and at 'em. It's Bippie time!"

"Bip this, you butt-hole," Alan Berman groaned.

He was in the bed next to Pacey's, and he pulled his pillow over his head just like Pacey did. All the other Bears, however, were instantly out of their beds, jumping into their swim trunks.

"Bippie time? Hooray!" Melvin shouted.

"Shut up, Smelly," Alan growled. "Lemme sleep."

"Hey, don't you guys want to brush your teeth?" Dawson asked, yawning as he got out of bed.

"Not before Bippie time," Melvin insisted.

"Yo man, you don't brush your teeth before *any* time," Walter told him.

Pacey felt a tap on his shoulder. "Pac-ee? Excuse, please. We are to water now," Jason said. "Bippie time."

The Bippies club had been a Camp Homeric tradition that Mr. Tack had decided to implement at Camp Takabec as well. The self-selected Bippies were those boys and girls who, every morning at the first notes of reveille, jumped out of bed, put on their swimsuits, ran down to the waterfront, and jumped into Capeside Bay. They swam around for a few moments and then jumped out.

As far as Pacey was concerned, being a Bippie ranked right up there with root canal and Marilyn Manson music. But, unfortunately, every single Bear except Alan had decided to be a Bippie.

The swim would happen every single day of the camp season, rain or shine, warm or cold, Mr. Tack had told his campers. At the end of the camp season, he promised, if a person had showed up and jumped in every morning, he or she would be entitled to take part in the annual Bippie banquet.

Mr. Tack had also decreed that, in the interest of camp morale, if even one camper from a bunk decided to be a Bippie, then at least one counselor from that bunk had to go to the waterfront and jump in too. Rain or shine.

"Dawson!" Pacey called from underneath his pillow. "It's your day, man. I suffered through it yesterday."

"I'm on it," Dawson assured him, yawning and shivering in the early-morning chill as he pulled on some cutoffs. "You guys ready?"

"We make to swim," Jason repeated.

"Jason, can I ask you something?" Pacey asked, without looking out from under his pillow

"I make answer to best of possibility," Jason replied.

"How did your name get to be Jason Phillips if you're from Slovakia? I'm just curious."

Pacey moved the pillow so he could see Jason's face. Jason thought for a moment, and then he understood the question. "Ah!" he exclaimed. "In home country, name is Janos Philippousis. Come to U.S.A., it make to be Jason Phillips."

Pacey nodded. "I'd do that too. Okay, Bippies, go with Dawson."

"In a minute," Caesar said. He was sitting on his bed, using an alcohol-based antibacterial cleanser on his hands. He carried the small plastic bottle with him everywhere he went.

"I don't think there are too many germs running around camp right now, Caesar," Dawson told him. "They're all still asleep."

"Let's go, man!" Walter yelled impatiently.

"Gonna do a cannonball, Walter?" Kenny asked. "If you do, we'll have a camp earthquake." Walter rushed to Kenny and belly-bumped him hard.

"You wanna say that again, fool?"

Andrew stood in the cabin doorway, clad in a terrycloth bathrobe over his bathing suit and thongs on his feet. "Maybe we could save the fighting until later," Andrew suggested. "It's counterproductive if it keeps us from getting down to the water promptly. And then Mr. Tack will bar us from the Bippie banquet at the end of the year."

"Casper is right," Kenny agreed. Two minutes later, the Bears, led by Dawson, were jogging down the dirt road that led to the waterfront. There were already a few dozen kids of both sexes there, standing at the water's edge or out on one of the pontoon docks.

Clad in a no-nonsense black racer-back swimsuit with camp shorts over it, Charma stood on a pontoon dock with a megaphone.

"All Bippies in the water!" she shouted into the megaphone. "Bippies, hit it!"

"Yahoo!" the Bears yelled, as they ran down to the beach and waded in. Dawson hung back, stretching. He definitely wasn't awake yet.

"Hey, Bippie," a female voice said from behind him. He turned. It was Sarah, Joey's co-counselor, looking muscular and fit in a royal blue bathing suit. "After what Joey told me about you, I didn't figure you for the Bippie type."

"I'm more the make-a-film-about-other-people-doing-it type," Dawson said. "But I have a feeling you're a serious swimmer."

"Yeah. But I don't mind hanging out with a rookie. You wanna go for it?"

Dawson grinned at her. "Sure." Together they ran down to the beach, out to the end of the dock, and jumped into the water, screaming at the top of their lungs.

"Woo, that feels so great!" Sarah cried happily, when she surfaced again.

"A bracing way to start the day," Dawson quipped.

"Hey, Dawson, is it deep out there?" Melvin called. He was splashing around in the shallow end with some of the eight- and nine-year-old boys. Dawson waved to him and Melvin happily waved back.

"Sweet kid, huh?" Sarah asked.

"Too sweet for the Bears," Dawson replied. "They eat their babies." She laughed, then did a surface dive. Dawson looked around. She popped up behind him and tapped him on the shoulder. He dog paddled to face her.

"Nice move," he said.

"Lots more where that came from. Listen, I didn't get to tell you how great your ghost story was the other night, the one about Witch Island. I wanted to tell you that night, but you seemed pretty busy with Gigi."

Dawson winced. "No. I was not busy with Gigi."

"Funny, that's not how it looked."

Dawson took in Sarah's fresh-faced beauty, clear

eyes, and direct, intelligent gaze. "Perceptions can be deceiving," he said.

"Interesting. So you and Gigi . . . ?"

Dawson shook his head.

A slow smile spread across Sarah's face. "Good. Joey told me a lot about you. And I am intrigued."

Dawson smiled back. But he couldn't help wondering just what Joey had told her. Especially what Joey had told her about Joey and Dawson.

"Smelly! Pass it to me!"

"No, to me!" Alan yelled. "Pass it to me before you get—"

Boom! A big kid from the Lions bunk stepped directly in front of Melvin, braced himself, and tackled the soccer ball away from him.

"Fool!" Walter yelled.

"Good try, Melvin!" Dawson called. He was playing goalkeeper for the Bears, which he didn't mind because it meant he wouldn't have to do a lot of running as the game progressed. At the other end of the field, one of the counselors for the Lions was doing the same thing. As for Pacey, he had pulled swim guard duty and was down at the waterfront. Trevor Braithwaite was acting as both coach and referee for the match, calling out encouragement as the boys played.

"Good going, Lyle," he yelled to the boy who had tackled Melvin and was now dribbling the soccer ball directly at Dawson. "Get up, Melvin, and give chase, lad, give chase!"

Dawson took his eye off the ball long enough to

see whether Melvin was getting to his feet. He was, but very, very slowly. Unenthusiastically, he started half-jogging toward the defensive end, as the Lions' attack bore in on Dawson.

"You stink, Smelly!" Alan yelled, holding his nose.

"Where's my defense?" Dawson cried at Jason Phillips and Andrew Casparian. "Go get 'em!"

"Go, Lions, go, Lions, go-o-o-o, Lions!" Gigi and her girls' cheerleading squad yelled from the sidelines. They were all of Andie's seven-year-olds.

Jason responded immediately, charging up to defend as Lyle still controlled the ball. As for Casper, he seemed to be busy examining something on the ground out by the stripe at the far end of the penalty area. He was easy to pick out because he wore a long-sleeved shirt, long pants, a wraparound sun visor, and a baseball cap to protect his pigmentless skin against the sun.

Jason, by far the best soccer player on the field, blocked Lyle's way, but he cleared the ball out the side where Casper should have been defending. Another Lion stood there. He one-timed a cross that sailed beautifully in front of the goal.

"Your ball, Lyle!" Trevor instructed. "Show it the back of the net!"

Do I try to make a grab for it? Dawson thought, knowing that as the goalkeeper he had the right to use his hands. *Or do I encourage the kid by letting him score a goal on me? In the larger existential scheme of things, what is the right thing for me to—*

Lyle leaped high in the air and executed a perfect

header on the ball, driving it to Dawson's right and into the net. Dawson couldn't have touched it if he'd wanted to.

"Lions roar, Lions score, g-o-o-o-o, Lions!" the cheerleaders bellowed.

"Jolly well done, lad!" Trevor exclaimed, blowing his whistle. "Time's up, that's the end of the game, Lions one, Bears nil! Bravo Lions, let's have a cheer!"

The Lions players all mobbed Lyle, who grinned at Dawson. Then they gave a hearty two-four-six-eight, who-do-we-appreciate cheer for the Bears. Meanwhile, the Bears stood around dejectedly.

"How come those girls never cheer for us?" Caesar asked, cutting his eyes to the cute girls on Gigi's squad.

"Probably because we're terrible," Kenny said. "Do you really want second graders cheering for you? They're a bunch of babies. And what is with that girl in charge of them?"

"Yo, what's up with the friendly ghost, man?" Walter asked. Everyone turned to look. Casper was still just standing there, looking at something on the ground. Trevor and Dawson both walked over to him.

"What are you doing, lad?" Trevor asked him. "You should have been defending on that last rush down the field."

"Look," Casper said with hushed reverence, pointing to a green insect on the field. "A praying mantis. They're fantastic insects. I stayed here when I saw it because I didn't want anyone to run over it in the game. Hey, look guys!" he called to his bunkmates. "A praying mantis!"

"Say *what?*" Walter sneered. Jason and Caesar came over to inspect the insect.

"Cool," Ceasar said.

Jason nodded. "Kewl."

Trevor looked at Casper. "But, lad, you can't do that. Your team is depending on you."

Andrew didn't say a word. He just reached down to pick up the insect. By this time, the rest of the Bears had wandered over to see what was going on. They gathered wordlessly around Andrew.

"It was just a game, Trevor," Andrew replied calmly. "By tomorrow, no one will remember the score. But if some of the players had stepped on this beautiful insect, it would be dead. And dead is forever." There was much head-nodding and mumbled agreement from the Bears.

"You know, Andrew, you're right," Dawson told him.

"But that's ridiculous, lad," Trevor protested. "It's just a bug!"

"He's making an excuse 'cuz they're such big losers!" one of the larger Lions yelled.

"No, it's not just a bug. It's a praying mantis. There's a difference. I'm taking it to the nature shack to show Ranger Chuck," Andrew told his bunkmates as he cradled the praying mantis in his hands. "And then I'm going to bring it back here. Catch and release, like in fishing."

"Great idea," Dawson told him. He crouched down so that he was on Andrew's level. "You don't want anything to hurt—"

"What, may I ask, are you doing?" Dawson and Andrew both looked up into the eyes of Mr. Tack.

"Andrew found a praying mantis while we were playing soccer and he didn't want anything to happen to it," Dawson explained. "He's planning to take it to the nature lodge. I think it's admirable on his part, don't you?"

Andrew looked at his bunkmates, who all nodded gravely. Then he looked to the camp director for his approval. "It's a beautiful insect. So powerful for its size. Don't you think so, Mr. Takermann?"

Mr. Tack glared at him. "It's a *bug*, Andrew."

"But—"

"I read your file from Camp Homeric, young man. Last summer you collected caterpillars and kept them in your cubby. You were too busy nursing some baby bird to take part in color war. But, I thought, another year's maturity. He's a smart kid. I bet he'll be a terrific addition to Takabec. You're disappointing me, Andrew."

Andrew hung his head. "I was only bringing it to the nature lodge."

"It seems to me that we should encourage the fact that different campers have different interests," Dawson told the camp director.

"Oh, do you?" The other campers watched, wide-eyed, as Mr. Tack's face grew beet red. "I watched that so-called soccer game—the last few minutes of it, anyway. I saw how the Lions scored on your squad, Dawson. You are the goaltender for a team of losers. Little losers grow up to be big losers. Is that what you want for your boys?"

Dawson held his ground. "I don't necessarily think a lack of interest in or talent for athletics means that someone is a loser, sir."

"Thank you for your highly evolved sentiments, Mr. Leery," Mr. Tack said sarcastically. "I realize you live in your own little bubble called Capeside, but these boys don't. It's a swim-with-the-sharks world out there and these boys will get eaten alive."

"But—" Dawson began. Mr. Tack held up his hand to silence him.

"Andrew's parents sent Andrew here to be under my supervision because they believe I am running the kind of institution from which their child can benefit. Son"—he turned to Andrew—"let that praying mantis go."

Andrew looked at the insect in his hand with something close to love. Dawson's heart went out to him. At the same time, he felt like putting his fist through the camp director's smug face.

"Go ahead, son," Mr. Tack said. "It's just a bug. It's not important." Caspar opened his hands, and the insect fell to the ground. A collective sigh escaped from the Bears.

"I sincerely hope Mr. Witter doesn't share your camping philosophy, Dawson," Mr. Tack told Dawson. "I'll be keeping a close eye on you two."

He turned to the Bears. "Boys, we've got our work cut out for us this summer. I want you to know that though you came into my camp pathetic losers, I'll do my best to see that you don't leave my camp pathetic losers. I believe in you boys. If you dream it, you can achieve it." His finger stabbed the air toward

Walter. "Suck in that gut, son. It's a disgrace. 'Bye for now. Great chatting with you, boys." The camp director strode away briskly.

"Butt-hole," Kenny mumbled, too ashamed to lift his face. There were more general murmurs of agreement.

"He's not Mr. Tack, he's Mr. Tacky," Andrew declared, dropping to his knees to pick up the praying mantis again. "I'm taking this to the nature lodge. Who wants to come with me?"

"I'm in," Walter declared, hitching up his gym shorts. Everyone else yelled that they would go with him too.

Dawson watched the little band of misfits trudge off toward the nature lodge. He realized, to his own surprise, that he liked them. He liked them a lot.

From the other direction Andie came walking over, holding the hand of a sobbing little girl. "It's okay, sweetie," Andie kept telling her. "Cheerleading's over for the day. We'll find your big brother and then you'll feel so much better."

"Problem?" Dawson asked her.

"Major. Darla, like the others, is a little young to be at sleep-away camp, and she has a little problem that involves changing her sheets at around 2 A.M. every morning and she's homesick and she wants her brother. She told me he's a Bear."

"You just passed them going in the other direction," Dawson told her.

"We did?" Andie knelt down. "Did you see your brother, Darla?" She shook her head and sobbed even harder.

Andie winced. "Didn't you tell me he's a Bear, sweetie?"

She shook her head again. "A ha-ha-hare," she managed.

"Ah. The nine-year-olds," Dawson explained.

"Great," Andie groaned.

"I want my brother," Darla moaned.

"Well, we'll just go find him," Andie said, trying to keep an encouraging smile on her face. "Whose idea was it for us to work here this summer?"

"Yours."

"That's what I thought."

Chapter 6

Attention All Campers!!!
Auditions for the Camp Play *Grease*
Today! 2–5 P.M.
No Prior Experience Necessary
Come and Join the Fun!!!

(sign in on the sign-in sheet when you arrive)

From where Pacey sat, slumped over in the last row of the playhouse, he could see the huge poster outside the open playhouse door encouraging campers to audition for the play. The good news was, from the large numbers of campers streaming in, it was clear that the concept of being in the camp play was a popular notion. The bad news was, by his count, there were only four boys.

"Nice turnout," Jen noted from her seat next to him.

"Yes," Pacey allowed. "If you're doing a production of *Little Women*. Has it escaped you that we are seriously underwhelmed by testosterone?"

"Little escapes me, Pacey, surely you know that by now." Jen tapped the eraser end of her pencil against the leg of her jeans as she surveyed the turnout. "We'll just have to indulge in a little creative casting."

"Gay *Grease*?" Pacey asked. "Instead of it taking place at Rydell High, we set it on the island of Lesbos?"

"Interesting concept," Jen replied, "but not exactly what I had in mind. It's common knowledge that a lot more girls go out for theater than guys. And it's common practice simply to cast some of the girls in guy roles."

"And you know this because—?"

Jen cocked her head at the kids mingling near the stage. "Because we have roughly thirty-two girls over there dying to be in this play, and four boys who look like they're facing a death sentence."

Pacey nodded. "Good point." He rolled himself out of the seat. "Well, no time like the present. Shall we?"

"We shall." The two of them walked to the front of the playhouse together and hopped up onto the stage.

"Hi, everyone!" Jen called over the excited voices of the kids. "If you could all just take a seat, we'd like to get started."

Most of the kids sat down, but a pale-faced, serious-looking girl approached them. She looked to be about thirteen. "Excuse me, my name is Tia, and Joey Potter is my day counselor," she told them. "She said she's a friend of yours."

"She is," Jen agreed.

"She said I should tell you that I had the lead in *Joan of Arc* at my school and I am very interested in getting the lead in this play."

"That's great, Tia, and it's great that you want to be in the play," Jen told her. "But we're going to have to let everyone audition before we know who—"

"Excuse me, but I only want to audition for Sandy," the girl interrupted, her hands in two tight little fists.

"Well, cool," Pacey said. "But I gotta tell you that being in the play is going to be a blast no matter what. It would be a shame if you only tried out for one role and didn't get it, because then you'd miss the fun of being in the play. See what I mean?"

She nodded, the look on her face even more grave. "But I just wanted to tell you that—"

"Sucking up, Tia?" a pretty girl with blond hair who looked at least sixteen but who Jen knew couldn't be older than fourteen jeered from her seat in the front row. "Did she tell you all about playing Joan of Arc yet?" The cute brunette next to her laughed as red splotches of embarrassment blossomed on Tia's cheeks. "If I could speak to you privately for a moment?" she asked. "Backstage?"

"We really don't have time right now," Jen told her.

"You can audition for anything you want, Tia." It was clear that the girl had more to say—probably a lot more, unfortunately, Jen was thinking—but she felt the best way to deal with too-earnest kids who wanted to suck up all your attention was to set boundaries right from the start.

As Tia slunk away, Jen and Pacey faced the rows of excited campers. "Great turnout," Jen told them, grinning. "For those of you who don't know us, I'm Jen, this is Pacey, and we're in charge of the drama program for the camp."

"How many of you are familiar with the play *Grease*?" Pacey queried. Almost every hand flew into the air.

"Great," Pacey said. "That makes it a lot easier. So listen, right up front we want you all to know that every single kid who wants to be in the play is going to be in the play, 'cuz here at Camp Takabec we stick together, right?"

He was met by abject silence. "Right!" Pacey answered himself. "Anyway, that means you don't have to be nervous when you audition, because you already know you're in."

A girl in the second row raised her hand. "Yes?" Jen asked.

"Well, what if you only want a good part? Last year I was in the chorus of *Oklahoma* and, no offense or anything, but it was kind of boring," the girl said.

"There's a famous saying," Jen told her. "There are no small parts, only small actors. Which means that every part is a good part and everyone's important, whether they have lots of lines or no lines."

"Well, what I mean is, can I drop out if I get like no lines?" she asked.

"You could," Pacey acknowledged slowly. "But it would be better if you just don't audition for a part that you're unwilling to accept in the first place, okay?"

"Okay."

"All right!" Jen rubbed her hands together enthusiastically. "Just by rough count, how many of you are interested in auditioning for Danny Zuko, the male lead?"

Three out of four of the boys raised their hands.

"And how many of you girls are interested in auditioning for Sandy, the female lead?" Jen asked.

Every single girl in the playhouse's hand shot into the air.

"Swell," Pacey said, a shade too brightly. "You guys know that all the girls in the Pink Ladies have really major parts, too, right? And, um . . . there are other great roles for girls, like Cha-Cha and Patti and Miss Lynch." A handful of girls nodded. Pacey and Jen traded looks. It was a playhouse full of Sandy wannabes.

Okay, we'll get the audition started then," Jen said. "The Camp Takabec playhouse audition rules are, no talking in the house during auditions, and everyone is respectful and supportive to everyone else, got it?"

Pacey turned to Jen. "Didn't you tell me that some counselor was supposed to be here to accompany these kids on piano for the audition?"

"Mr. Tack told me he had a counselor who would play for auditions and for the show," Jen confirmed. "He didn't tell me who it was, but—"

"There's no business like show business, eh lads?"

Trevor called out as he strode into the playhouse. " 'Lo, kids. Ready to rock 'n' roll?"

"Hi, Trev," the pretty blond said to him, her voice a sexy purr.

"Hey, Britney, how goes it?" Trevor called back easily. "You're trying out for Sandy?"

"You play piano?" Pacey asked as Trevor athletically hopped up onto the stage.

"Well, I'm no Glenn Gould, but I've been known to tickle the ivories. Great to see you, Jen."

"Soccer, football, piano," Jen listed on her fingers. "Aren't you the Renaissance man."

He leaned close. "I have qualities that would surprise you, darlin'."

Pacey regarded him. "Frankly, the unbridled ego thing is way too obvious."

"Good one," Trevor said, laughing as he headed for the piano, which was stage right.

At least he's a good-natured egomaniac, Pacey thought.

"Okay, listen up!" Jen called. "You all should have signed in on the list by the door and you'll be auditioning in the order in which you signed in. You'll be singing first; then you'll be reading a scene as the character you'd like to play. Did you all get copies of the scenes from the pile by the door?"

There were nods all around. "Cool," Jen said. "About the singing part. You can sing something from *Grease,* or 'Happy Birthday,' or whatever makes you comfortable. Trevor has the score from *Grease* but if you want to sing something else, ask him if he knows it, or you can sing a cappella."

"What's that?" a little girl in the front asked.

"A resort town in Mexico," Britney replied sarcastically.

The girl smiled innocently. "Oh yeah, my parents went there on their honeymoon!" Britney and some of the older girls cracked up.

"Actually it means 'without accompaniment,' " Jen explained, shooting Britney a look that definitely said I-am-so-wise-to-your-games. But from the way Britney tossed her head and stared right back, it was clear that she didn't care.

"Okay, first on the sign-up sheet is Jennifer Monday," Pacey called as he and Jen went to sit in the front row. A skinny girl with a mouthful of braces walked up onstage. She was so nervous, it looked as if her whole body was shaking.

"Hi, Jennifer," Jen called warmly, trying to put the kid at ease. "We have the same name, huh?" She nodded.

"What would you like to sing, Jennifer?" Pacey asked.

" 'Happy Birthday'?" she asked fearfully.

"That would be fine," Pacey told her. "You want Trevor to play it while you sing?"

"Um . . . no." She screwed her eyes shut tight and began to sing. Out came a wispy little voice with a tenuous grasp on pitch.

"That was great," Jen told her when she'd finished. "And you want to try out for the role of—?"

"Sandy."

Pacey hopped back onstage. "I'll read Danny with you, okay?" She blushed furiously and nodded. They read the scene together, where Danny discovers that the girl he fell for over the summer has transferred to his school. Jennifer had a hard time reading, much less acting. Her hands were sweating so much that Pacey could see the pages she was holding were actually damp.

"That was terrific," Jen told her when they'd finished the scene. "Is there another role you'd like to audition for?"

The little girl's face fell. "Does that mean I didn't get it?"

"No," Jen said, "we'll be asking everyone that question. And also this one: Will you accept a non-speaking chorus role?" Jennifer nodded, but she looked crestfallen.

"Thanks, Jennifer," Pacey called to the girl as she trudged offstage.

After that, the auditions became something of a blur. Some kids were marginally better than Jennifer. Some were not. "Just a wild guess on my part," Pacey murmured to Jen, "but I don't think the next Gwyneth is spending the summer of her life here at Camp Takabec."

"Well, we just came to our first guy, number twenty. Maybe we'll luck out. Ricky McGee!" Jen called. A gangly kid who looked like a junior Ichabod Crane jumped up from his seat.

"Me, that's me," he said. He took the stairs up to the stage two at a time. "Can you play 'YMCA'?" he asked Trevor.

"I think I could make a stab at that," Trevor said, noodling the chords out as he spoke. "About like that?"

"Yeah, great!"

"Whenever you're ready, Ricky," Pacey called. Ricky began to sing the disco hit by the Village People as Trevor joined in on the piano. When he got to the chorus, he posed as each letter: Y-M-C-A.

In the back of the playhouse, Britney, who was now the gang leader for about a half-dozen girls, started to do it with him. Then her friends joined in, just to goof on him.

"Great . . . enthusiasm, Ricky," Jen told him, when he was finished. She climbed onstage. "I'll read Sandy with you, okay?"

Ricky blushed the color of overripe tomatoes. The scene was painful. On top of everything else, Ricky's voice was changing. Unfortunately, it was getting higher, not lower. A headache began to pound between Jen's eyes. If they didn't hit someone—anyone—with talent soon, the camp play was going to be the camp disaster.

When she and Pacey reached auditioner number twenty-seven, they found it was none other than Britney. She handed Trevor the sheet music to "Hopelessly Devoted to You."

"It's from the movie, not the play," she explained. "When the camp play was announced, I had my mother send it just in case you didn't know it."

"Smart girl," Trevor told her, centering the sheet music on his stand. "But I know it."

Britney took center stage as if she'd been born there. And she looked fantastic. Everyone in the playhouse stopped whatever they were doing to watch her. She began to sing. Her voice was all right—at least she hit all the notes—and it was loud. She acted out the song as it went along. From Jen and Pacey's perspective, it was clear that she'd copied every move from Whitney-Mariah-Celine, with a little bad Shirley Temple thrown in for good measure. For example, every time she hit the word "you" at the end of the line "hopelessly devoted to you," she gestured out at the audience, palm up.

"I think she's been studying the Miss America talent comp," Jen told Pacey. "Prelims for the prelims."

"You mean the horrid little hand gestures?" Pacey asked. "Can't we just cut off her hands?"

Jen nodded and Britney finished her song. The kids in the playhouse burst into applause. Pacey went up to read the scene with her. She was just as mannered and over-the-top in her acting as she'd been in her singing. It was clear, though, from the mesmerized looks on the kids' faces, that they thought she was all that and a bag of designer chips. It was also clear, from her attitude as she walked off-stage, that she figured she had the lead sewn up.

Following Britney there were a few halfway decent girls, though Jen had to admit that Britney was far and away the best. They'd just have to work with her on giving up all that fake stuff that she thought was acting. Maybe Dawson would have some tips on how to work with her.

Finally, they called the last boy who had signed up, Brad Snyder. He was fourteen, but looked older. In fact, he was by far the least geeky guy who was auditioning. Brad sang "Happy Birthday" loudly and off-key. He read the scene with Jen. His acting was just as over the top as Britney's.

"At least they'd look good together," Pacey mumbled to Jen when his audition was done.

"The under-fifteens think so too," Jen agreed reluctantly, cocking her chin toward the girls at the back of the playhouse. They looked ready to swoon at Brad's Nikes. Jen took a look at Brad. He was strutting around like he was John Travolta.

A perfect match with Britney, Jen thought. *Even though the idea of working with them for the next few weeks makes me want to gag.*

"Thanks Brad," Jen called as the kid swaggered off to talk with Britney.

"Well, last but not least," Jen looked at the bottom of the list. "Tia?" she called.

"I forgot all about that kid," Pacey said.

Tia walked over to them and handed them her computer-printed acting résumé, which consisted of her middle school acting credits and a chorus role in a community theater production of *Fiddler on the Roof.*

"How'd you end up last, Tia?" Jen asked.

"I planned it that way," she admitted. "So that you'd have a basis for comparison. Maybe you want to take a break, so that you're fresh for when I—"

"I think we're fine," Jen told her. "What are you going to sing?"

" 'There Are Worse Things I Could Do.' I know it's Rizzo's song, but I feel that it shows off my range better."

Jen and Pacey tried to keep a straight face as Tia climbed onto the stage. She began to sing. Her voice was . . . nice. No, it was really nice. She seemed to get more confident as she went on, and then it became *really* nice. Plus, she actually seemed to be connecting to the lyrics, which was a first in the afternoon's audition.

When she was done, Pacey went to read with her, but she stopped him. "If you don't mind, I've prepared a monologue."

"Give me a major break," Britney sneered, loud enough for Jen to hear.

"Quiet, please," Jen called sharply. "That's fine, Tia. Go ahead."

"It's from a play I wrote," she added with the utmost seriousness.

"Which she performed last season on Broadway with Scott Speedman," Britney's friend Kendall commented. Tia ignored her and began her monologue. It was all about a girl auditioning for a school play. She had clearly been the most talented actress, but the drama teacher picked someone else for the lead because the other girl was so much cuter and cooler. Tia's acting was very intense.

Pacey leaned toward Jen. "How much does she remind you of a little Andie? I wanna wrap her up and protect her from the Britneys of the world." Jen nodded her agreement.

"Okay, Tia, thanks," Pacey called to her when she'd finished. "Excellent, really."

Her face lit up. "Really?"

"Really-really," he assured her.

"Thanks." She headed for the stairs.

"Hey, wait a minute," Britney objected. "We all had to read from the script, so she should have to read from the script too. It's only fair." There were mumbles of agreement from the other girls in the playhouse.

"I believe that's my cue," Pacey told Jen.

"It is. But you realize that regardless of who we cast as Sandy, we are at minus zero for a Danny," Jen pointed out to him. "We have two ten-year-olds, Ricky, who seems to be in reverse puberty, and the Sean Penn wannabe who can't carry a tune."

"No choice. Gotta go with Brad, Mr. Sean Penn wannabe," Pacey said.

Jen groaned. "Maybe if we try to recruit more—"

"Yo, yo, yo, yo still doin' that play thing?" a voice boomed out from the doorway. It was one of Pacey's campers, Walter Carrier. He was sweaty from head to toe and carried a football.

Brad laughed. "What happened, fat boy, try to eat the entire camp for lunch?"

Walter swaggered his hefty body over to Brad. "I just came from football, my boys lost, and I'm feelin' moody. I don't think you wanna be messin' with me, fool."

Brad cracked up. "Who are you supposed to be, fat, white Puff Daddy?"

"Cut it out you two," Jen called sharply, "or both your butts are out of here. Got it?"

Walter turned to Pacey. "Cut me some slack, man. I was playin' and the counselor said I couldn't leave. That's why I'm late and like that."

Pacey vaguely recalled that the kid liked to sing. And even though he was only ten, he was so big for his age that he was at least as tall as any girl who had auditioned. He looked over at Jen, who nodded.

"Fine, whatever. Go for it," Pacey told Walter.

He climbed up onstage. "Want me to play for you, Walt?" Trevor asked.

"You know 'Unchained Melody'?"

Trevor shrugged. "Sorry."

"That's cool. I can sing without you playing." He turned to the audience and began to sing. He was great.

"Yes!" Jen stage-whispered to Pacey, when he was only halfway into the song. "Do you hear that?"

Pacey nodded. "He's like a flashback to Meatloaf, circa *Rocky Horror*."

"Now why aren't we doing that as the camp play? Anyway, I *love* this kid!" Jen hissed.

When Walter finished singing, Jen read with him. He was young, of course, but sweet and honest. And he knew all about Danny's fake swagger, because he did the same thing himself, all the time.

When they were finished, Jen sighed with relief. Auditions were over. She and Pacey told the kids that the cast list would be posted before breakfast at the dining hall bulletin board, and the kids all wandered out. Jen stretched her neck, plopped down in a chair, and then draped her legs over Pacey. "I'm beat," she said. "So, what do you think?"

"I think Walter kicked butt," Pacey said, grinning. "And frankly, I'm wallowing in a moment of fatherly pride."

"He's our Danny, then," Jen agreed. "And for Sandy?"

"Britney's got the look, no question," Pacey acknowledged.

Jen folded her arms pensively. "Tia was so much more honest, though."

"Can I put my two cents in?" Trevor asked, coming out from behind the piano to join them.

"Oh, sure," Jen told him. "What do you think?"

"I'm going to tell you something a certain girl told me in confidence," Trevor began. "This certain girl-who-shall-remain-nameless confessed to me that in fact she didn't play the lead in her school's production of *Joan of Arc*. A pretty girl got the part instead. This girl-who-shall-remain-nameless wrote a monologue about it. And, might I add, this girl is hand-over-fist superior, in this case, to the pretty girl."

Jen regarded Trevor with something beyond hormonal interest for the first time. "Why, Trevor, I do believe a soul is lurking under that flip exterior."

He winked. "Don't let it get around."

"I think we have our two leads," Pacey said. "Walter and Tia."

Jen smiled. "Britney and Brad are going to be so pissed." She put her hands behind her head and laced her fingers together. "I, for one, am going to enjoy every moment of it."

Chapter 7

"**A**ndie! Check out my painting!" As soon as she saw Andie come into the arts and crafts house, Lillith held up a finger painting she'd just completed, every color of which was also on her shorts, T-shirt, and face.

"It's great, Lillith," Andie told her.

"Not as nice as mine. Look at mine, Andie," Darla insisted, holding hers up.

"Great," Andie said, keeping a smile plastered to her face.

"And yours too," she added hastily, knowing the twins, Maya and Toni, would also want praise for their artwork. All the girls were just as paint-covered as Lillith was.

"Sorry, I know they're kind of a mess," Joey told Andie. "But they got bored with making pots and begged to fingerpaint. They wore me down."

"I'm sure you intend to compensate for that error in judgment by volunteering to help me shower and shampoo the little angels, right?" Andie asked sweetly.

"Right," Joey reluctantly agreed. "Sounds swell."

"Wash your hands in the sink, girls," Andie told them. "Then we'll head over to the dining room for snack time, and then we'll go shower and take an afternoon nap, okay?"

"Will you read us *The Why Book*?" Darla begged. "Please?"

"But I've read you guys *The Why Book* every single day. Maybe you'd like a different book—"

No, no, no, they all insisted, making the din that only four overindulged seven-year-olds could make. "Fine," Andie snapped. *"The Why Book."* The girls traipsed over to the sink to wash their hands.

"What's *The Why Book*?" Joey asked as she began putting the art supplies away.

"It began with the midget she-devil from hell, Darla, over there," Andie replied confidentially, her voice low so that the girls wouldn't hear her. "She asked me what the scientific reason was that Toni and Maya had brown skin. It seems that little Darla's parents never explained pigment to her. I found this book at the Capeside library. Why is the sky blue? Why do people have different color skin? That kind of thing. For some reason they just love this book. Probably because their parents aren't around enough to answer these kinds of questions."

Joey thought a moment. "Tragically, I don't know the answer to those questions."

Andie grabbed a sponge to help sponge down the

tables. "Well, since you'll be with us for shower time, you can stay for naptime and find out."

"Lucky me."

"Andie, Maya just pushed me. On purpose," Darla declared, holding her right arm as if it were broken. It wasn't.

"My drama queen," Andie told Joey. She went over to Darla. "Let me see it, sweetie."

"I need candy to make me feel better," Darla insisted. "It calms me down." She turned to Maya. "Next time you touch me, I'm calling my father. He's a lawyer."

"We're talking seriously overtired," Andie told Joey. "I'm gonna take them for snacks and then head back before they all start picketing. Meet me there?"

"As soon as I finish cleaning up," Joey promised.

"Great. Okay guys, let's go." Maya grabbed Andie's right hand and Lillith grabbed her left hand. Then the two other girls held on to her legs. With all four paint-covered girls clinging to her, Andie tried to make it out the door just as Dawson was on his way in.

"Looks like you've got your hands full," Dawson observed.

"If every girl spent a summer in this job, the teen pregnancy rate would drop to nothing," Andie observed grimly.

Dawson turned to watch Andie stumble down the path with the kids. "And I thought I had it tough with the Bears."

"Were we that obnoxious at that age?" Joey asked him as she wrung out the oversized sponge in the sink.

"Probably worse."

"So, how was film club today?" Joey asked. "Got any budding Dawsons on your hands?"

"Actually, Jason—the kid who barely speaks a word of English—seems to have a true affinity for it. He's making a sort of documentary about the Bears. He videos them all the time. It's really amazing, how the medium of film transcends the language barrier."

"Next thing you know he'll be submitting it to Sundance and then he'll be crowned the Slovak Harmony Korine." She threw him a sponge. "If you're here, you help."

Dawson tackled some blobs of red and blue paint under a table. "In my admittedly subjective and exceedingly biased opinion, the kids in Andie's bunk have more talent than Harmony Korine."

"You know what I think of him. First we snuck in to see *Kids* and then I hated it so much that I snuck out," Joey reminded him.

"Not to change the subject, but I wanted to run something by you," Dawson said.

"I'm all ears. And paint smudges."

"It is common knowledge that Mr. Tack—also known as Mr. Tacky, the Tackman, or the Tackmeister—hates the kids in my bunk. I mean, he has a true antipathy for them. It's driving me crazy."

"Does it bother your kids?" Joey asked.

"Of course it does. Not that they'd let on. I mean, they fully realize they are already the least cool bunk at camp. Acknowledging that being belittled by the camp director on a daily basis hurts your feelings would only ensure their place as permanent outcasts."

"Maybe you should talk this over with Mr. Tack," Joey suggested.

"Oh, come on, Joey. The man is about as open to constructive criticism as James Cameron. There's really nothing I can do to change the situation. I grow more and more frustrated every day, and I feel like I'm just watching my summer fritter away."

"So what are you saying, Dawson? You want to quit?"

He sighed and leaned against the wall. "I don't know. Is that what I'm saying?"

"Well, if you quit, Mr. Tack would still dis the Bears, right?" Joey threw the sponge in the sink and wiped her hands off with a paper towel. "Only now, in addition to everything else, he'd tell them that their counselor thought they were such losers that he quit camp."

Dawson groaned. "That is a highly unpleasant scenario. Plus, Pacey would probably kill me for leaving him in the lurch. Not to mention how much I'd be letting those kids down. At least if I'm here I can make a feeble attempt to protect them from the Tackman's slings and arrows."

Joey smiled. "Sounds like you already have your answer, Dawson."

He went to her and gave her a hug. "Thanks."

"Hey, what are buds for?"

"Oh, sorry, am I interrupting?" Trevor stood in the doorway.

"No. We're old friends." Joey moved away from Dawson and self-consciously pushed some hair behind her ear. Dawson definitely did not like being classified as an "old friend." He also didn't like Trevor showing up at the art cabin.

"So, Trevor, what brings you to Fingerpainting 101?" Dawson asked.

Trevor pointed at Joey and flashed his disarming grin. "Thought you might be up for a sail," he told Joey.

Joey thought a moment. "I promised Andie I'd help her with something, but it'll only take maybe thirty minutes."

"Meet you down at the dock in half an hour, then?" Trevor asked.

Joey smiled. "All right. That sounds nice." Trevor gave Dawson a jaunty salute as he strode out of the cabin.

"What's that about?" Dawson asked Joey.

"It's called friendship, Dawson. Surely you've heard of it."

"Trevor doesn't strike me as the kind of guy who cultivates platonic relationships with beautiful girls, Joey."

Joey just shrugged. "Well, Dawson, I guess I'm about to find that out for myself."

"Football is played as much in your head as it is on the field," Jack told his young charges, who were gathered around him. It was already two weeks into the camp season, and things were in full swing. The twenty-one guys—and one girl—who were at morning football clinic had all signed up for football as a season-long elective sport. Usually there were twenty-two guys, but Walter was excused for play practice.

Jacks eyes slid over to Cassie Myers. She had short dark hair and a fabulous, sweet smile. She was twelve years old, about five-one, maybe a hundred and ten pounds. And she was a terrific, fearless athlete. The guys had given her a hard time since day one. But she'd hung in there, refusing to quit. Jack couldn't help but admire her spirit.

Besides, he knew just what it felt like to be the one who was different.

"Here's the thing," Jack went on, his eyes scanning the group. "There are always going to be physical mistakes. You'll try to tackle a guy and miss. You'll slip on wet ground. You'll be beaten trying to protect your quarterback. These things happen—physical mistakes. But who can give me an example of a mental mistake?"

Roger Repoz, a burly fourteen-year-old, raised his hand. "Yeah, Roger?"

Roger pointed to Cassie. *"She* is a mental mistake."

"And you are a mental midget," Cassie shot back.

"What are you gonna do about it?" Roger jeered. "Kick my butt?"

"We've already talked about this issue how many times?" Jack asked impatiently.

"So, she should just quit then," Roger insisted.

"My dad said that guys aren't supposed to tackle girls," his friend Pete added. "How am I supposed to play if I can't tackle her?"

"You can tackle me," Cassie said in frustration. "I *want* you to tackle me."

"Woo-woo," the guys' razzed. Roger stood up and

wiggled his butt, then walked around with a limp wrist and pursed lips.

Jack saw red. The kids had no idea he was gay. It was definitely more than they needed to know. So he had to find a way other than using himself as an example to get them to accept Cassie as one of them.

"Girls can be just as athletic as guys can," Jack said, trying to keep his tone even. "How would you like it if someone excluded you from what you wanted to do, just because you're a guy?"

Roger shrugged indifferently. Jack looked around as he tried to come up with another tack. On the sidelines, Gigi's cheerleading squad was currently practicing a routine. "Be aggressive, be-ee aggressive, kick 'em, hound 'em, knock 'em out, they'll be yours without a doubt, go Bears, go Bears, go-ooo Bears!" Two of the younger girls did a series of cartwheels while the older girls did aerial splits; then they all landed in a diamond formation.

It gave Jack an idea. "See those girls?" He cocked his head toward the cheerleaders. "Those girls are really strong athletes. It takes flexibility, gymnastic ability, strength training—"

"And a great rack," Simon Scott, a precocious ten-year-old, yelled, which cracked all the guys up again.

Cassie jumped to her feet, dark eyes flashing. "If you dis the cheerleaders, then you don't know anything about cheerleading. It's a sport as much as football."

The guys hooted derisively.

"You guys are just . . . just Neanderthals," Cassie spat.

"What's that?" Simon asked.

"Let's just chill on the name-calling, okay?" Jack said. "You're entitled to your own opinion about things, but you're not entitled to dis anyone else at this camp. Got it?"

His question was greeted with silence. "I'll take that as a yes," Jack said dryly. "Back to the subject at hand. No one gave me a *serious example* of a mental mistake. Let me give you one. A mental mistake is being distracted by something stupid on the field, like what your opponent says to you, instead of paying attention to the game. Now, on your feet, form two double lines on the fifty-yard stripe. Cassie, put your helmet on and come join me."

The campers did what Jack told them. In moments, there was a double line of players on the fifty-yard line, and Cassie stood with Jack at one end.

He handed her the football. "Cassie, run the gauntlet. On my whistle."

Cassie's eyes grew wide. She was a great athlete and had played football since she was a little kid, but there were guys on the gauntlet who outweighed her by sixty or seventy pounds.

"They'll kill me, Jack," Cassie told him. "They hate me."

"Your point being?"

Cassie looked taken aback. "I didn't think the point of the game was to literally *die.*"

Jack folded his arms. "Anyone on the team you're playing is going to play like he or she hates you, if they want to win. You're the one who wants to play football. And I respect that."

"But—"

"Believe me, I know what it's like to not have people accept you, Cassie," Jack told her, his voice low. "And I know something else too. You can lick your wounds and give up, or you can show 'em what you're made of."

Jack took the ball back from her. "It comes down to this. Are you going to run the gauntlet or are you going to just give up, walk away, and let them win?"

Cassie's chin jutted out. "Just give me the damn ball." Jack tossed it to her.

"Be aggressive, be-ee aggressive!" Gigi's cheerleaders started anew on their cheer. Jack blew a blast on his whistle loud enough to make the cheerleaders stop in the middle of the routine.

"Gigi, can your girls to knock it off?" Jack called. "My players are trying to concentrate!"

"So are my cheerleaders," Gigi called back. "What do your players plan to do when we cheer at an actual game?"

"When it's an actual game there'll be fans yelling to drown out your cheerleaders," Jack replied.

Gigi's pom-poms flew to her hips. "That is so not funny." She glared at him, but ordered her girls to work on their tumbling instead of their cheering.

Jack turned back to Cassie. "Ready?" She nodded, grim-faced.

"Ready on the gauntlet?" Jack asked his players.

"Ready, coach!" came a mass cry from the two lines of football players. Jack gave another shrill blast on the whistle, and Cassie, grasping the ball to her chest with both hands, plunged into the gauntlet. For the next couple of seconds, the only sounds on the field were the smashing of shoulder pad against shoulder pad and body against body as the two lines of the gauntlet converged on the girl with the ball.

She made it halfway through before a fierce hit from Roger on one side and one of the other fourteen-year-olds on the other smacked her to the ground. She fell, the ball popping loose and skittering crazily away from her.

From Gigi's crew of cheerleaders on the sidelines came the bray of derisive laughter. Some of the guys on the team joined in.

"The next guy on this team who laughs is on permanent suspension!" Jack yelled as he hurried to Cassie's side to make sure the girl hadn't been hurt. She hadn't. Jack told her to get up and do it again.

Boom! Same result, this time after Cassie made it a third of the way down the gauntlet. But this time only the cheerleaders laughed, the guys on the team were silent.

"Come try out for cheerleading!" Kendall called out through cupped hands. "That is, if you think you can cut it!"

"Just a little tip," Britney yelled. "Looks count!"

Most of the younger cheerleaders cracked up as Cassie lay on the ground, sucking air.

"You okay?" Jack asked.

"Winded, that's all," she managed.

"Then get up."

"Coach—"

"I mean it, Cassie," Jack ordered. He tossed the football to another counselor who was helping him run the drills. "Roger Repoz, you're on the gauntlet. I need to talk to my player." He reached down and helped Cassie to her feet, then led her until they were standing together twenty or thirty yards from the gauntlet.

"How do you feel?" Jack asked her.

"Like a bunch of guys pummeled me," Cassie said, gritting her teeth. There was a clod of turf literally stuck in the face mask of her helmet. "My thigh hurts and my arm hurts and I basically can't breathe. But I'm still standing."

"You want to take a break?"

"Yeah," she admitted gratefully.

"Well, forget it," Jack snapped. "How tough are you?"

"But they're killing me out there, Coach. It's because I'm a girl."

Jack looked over at his players. "Let me tell you something. I didn't start football until this past season. When I started, the guys on my team kicked my butt when I ran the gauntlet."

"Because you were the new guy?"

"Something like that," Jack replied. "I didn't like it. In fact, I wanted to quit. But I didn't. Because there's always something, Cassie. You're too tall or too short or too fat or too skinny or too *whatever*. That doesn't matter. Let me tell you what matters: to get to the end of gauntlet, to get to the end of the line. That's it. You either do it or you don't. The choice is yours."

Cassie toed the grass of the field uncomfortably as Jack waited. Finally, she looked up at him again and held her hand out. "Give me the ball."

He did. The cheerleaders began jeering again. "WWF needs you!" Britney heckled Cassie. Jack glared at Gigi, but she made no move to stop the catcalling.

A blast from Jack's whistle brought order to the gauntlet. "Tacklers ready?" he called.

"Ready!" the players grunted.

"Go!" he yelled to Cassie. The girl charged into the gauntlet, and, as before, the air was full of the harsh sounds of pads on pads and crunching bodies. And, as before, Cassie found herself slammed to the ground. This time, though, she'd made it three-quarters of the way down the double line of boys, and this time she'd held on to the football.

"Good job, Cassie!" Jack called as the girl bounced immediately to her feet. He looked at his watch. "Okay, let's take a water break. Back on the field in ten minutes."

Jack and the players, including Cassie, drifted off the field toward the sidelines, where Gigi had resumed her cheerleading drills. When Gigi saw the football players coming, she called a break for her charges as well. The boys and girls mingled near the water fountain, and Jack jogged over to an equipment shed to pick up some traffic cones to use in his next drill, leaving his players behind.

Cassie drank thirstily from the drinking fountain as Britney and Kendall sauntered over to her. "Excuse me," Kendall began, "but there's a rumor going around that you had a sex change operation and we just wanted to know if that's true."

Cassie lifted her head from the water fountain. "What's your problem?"

"I don't have the problem, sweetie," Britney said. "You do."

"I didn't know that brains were in such short supply when they gave yours out," Cassie snapped.

"Ooh," Britney said. "I am just so hurt. Is all this hostility because no boy asked you out at the fifth-grade dance or something?"

"I'm in seventh, for your information," Cassie told her.

"I am so sorry that I mistook you for a fifth grader, I really am," Britney said. "You might want to ask mom to make that doctor's appointment, get the old hormonal imbalance thing checked out."

Gigi walked over to them. "That's enough," she told Britney.

"But Brit was just trying to help her, girl power and all that," Kendall insisted.

"Why don't you leave that to me?" Gigi suggested. "Cassie, may I talk to you for a moment?"

Cassie nodded. Gigi put an arm around her. "Walk with me for a bit, 'kay?" They began strolling toward the far goal line.

"You know those girls don't mean anything by what they're saying," Gigi told Cassie. "They're only kidding."

"It wasn't very funny."

"Well, sweetie, look at yourself," Gigi said gently. "Wearing a boy's uniform, with gigantic shoulder pads. Now, I myself like the shoulder pad look in moderation, with the right outfit, but plastic ones are just a little excessive, don't you think?"

"It's not for fashion," Cassie said. "If you don't wear them, you can get hurt."

94

"And I would truly hate for that to happen," Gigi said. "Honey, girls shouldn't be playing football. It's dangerous. And it's not very feminine. Just look at you—you're a sweaty mess. But under that sweaty mess is a very pretty girl who can potentially grow up to become a beautiful young woman. You could be so cute and popular and have so many friends! I'd like to help you to achieve that goal so that one day you can—"

"Gigi, shut up."

Gigi and Cassie both looked behind them. Jack stood there with his arms folded, his face a mask of fury.

"Beg your pardon?" Gigi asked.

"Gigi," Jack began, his tone steely, "maybe if you had played football when you were a girl you would have something other than the pathetic lack of character that you currently demonstrate."

"You don't even know me," Gigi sputtered.

"True. And I don't want to," Jack said.

"I hope you realize that you are ruining this girl's life. She needs a role model and a mentor, not you." Gigi turned to Cassie. "I'm here for you, sweetie, if you need me." She stormed off toward her girls on the sideline.

"You okay?" Jack asked.

There were tears in Cassie's eyes, but she clenched her teeth and didn't let them fall. "Give me the ball, and get the gauntlet out on the field. Let's do it again."

Chapter 8

Jen stood on the high-diving board dock, a twenty-foot cane pole in her hands as forty or so girls frolicked in the deep water of Capeside Bay. Camp Takabec was on the buddy system, which meant that all kids in the water had to swim with a buddy nearby. When Charma blew her whistle—sometimes Jen thought that life itself would be impossible at Camp Takabec without the invention of the whistle—all the swimmers would buddy up and Jen would count the couples.

Not exactly a mental challenge, she thought, squinting into the afternoon sun.

"Hey, Jen, watch this!"

Jen looked up. One of her favorite campers, Cara Himmelfarb, a twelve-year-old with the reddest, curliest hair Jen had ever seen, took three steps to the end of the high dive, launched herself out and upward, then sliced toward the water in a beautiful swan dive.

"Way to go, Cara!" Jen told her when the girl's head popped above the water.

"Big deal, she gets lessons every day during the school year," Alexis, another girl in Jen's bunk, announced to everyone on the dock. "Her family is megarich."

"She still has to go to the lessons and do the work," Jen pointed out.

"If you saw the guy who teaches her, you'd understand," Alexis said. "Total fox material."

On the main dock, Charma blew her whistle twice, long and loud. Jen winced as the shrill sound echoed in her ears. The whistle was the signal for all campers to buddy up, which they did. Jen counted the swimmers. Then she put her right hand in the air in the "okay" sign, meaning that everyone was present and accounted for. Then Charma gave two final blasts of her whistle, which meant that general swim was over.

It was a really warm afternoon. Jen wiped some sweat off her brow with the back of her arm, then replaced her rescue pole in its holder on the diving board. Once all the kids were out of the water, she dove in. It was cold, and it felt great. But play rehearsal started in twenty minutes, and she wanted to go over some notes with Pacey before they started.

She smiled to herself as she swam over to the main dock and boosted herself out of the water. After their initial nervousness over getting the leads in the play,

Walter and Tia had committed to working on the play as if it were their Broadway debut. It drove Britney and Brad, playing the second leads—Rizzo and Kenickie—absolutely crazy to watch the ten-year-olds rehearse. They'd even staged a confrontation where they and their friends insisted to Jen and Pacey that having little kids in the leads looked so stupid that everyone would laugh at the play before it even started. Jen and Pacey had hung tough, though privately, they both wondered at times if they'd done the right thing.

Jen padded over to Charma's lifeguard stand, where she'd left her terrycloth robe, and put it on. Huh. She felt something in her pocket that hadn't been there before. She pulled it out—a folded-up piece of paper. Her name was written on the outside in bold capital letters. She opened it. It was a hand-written note.

To the fairest of them all, Jen Lindley—
Trevor Braithwaite requests the honour of your presence this evening at the Coffee Café, corner of Main Street and Ocean Avenue in bucolic Capeside, at the hour of 9:30 P.M. R.S.V.P. necessary only for regrets. Mister Braithwaite shall await you with bated breath.

—TREVOR

Jen smiled. Well, well, well. The English soccer player was making his move. It appeared the summer was about to heat up quite nicely.

* * *

The Coffee Café had opened right after school had let out for the summer. The space had previously been a luncheonette that had gone out of business. There were two rooms: the large, main room where musicians sometimes performed, and the game room next door, with chess, checkers, darts, backgammon, etcetera. It was furnished with mismatched overstuffed chairs and ancient couches salvaged from Salvation Army.

A sign on the door of the Coffee Café read Open Mike Night. Jen opened the door to the packed café. Over the din of the crowd, she was hit with a warbling female voice accompanied by guitar. In the rear corner, a girl with long brown hair and multiple facial piercing stood on a small stage, strumming her guitar and crooning into the mike.

> *You said you loved me for myself*
> *Until I pierced my tongue*
> *You told me it was ugly*
> *So I knew you weren't the one . . .*

"Looking for anyone in particular?" Trevor asked, grinning, as he sauntered over to her, coffee mug in hand.

"A certain gentleman issued a written invitation," Jen replied. "Very quaint. How could I turn it down?"

"Indeed," Trevor agreed. "I've staked us out a table back there."

"Is it anywhere near the pierced Alanis wannabe?"

Trevor laughed. "Other side of the room, love." He took her hand and led her through the crowd.

*You said you'd never leave me
Until the truth of me unwound
A girl with stretch marks on her heart
Lost in the lost and found.*

The singer dropped her head dramatically as she struck the final chord of her dirge. A group of people—obviously her friends—stood up to whistle and applaud.

"Why does it seem like all chick songwriters want to do is slit their own wrists?" Jen asked as she and Trevor squeezed into the banquette against the far wall.

"Because 'I'm really happy and getting laid on a regular basis' doesn't sell quite as well as existential angst. I'll go get you a coffee. Capeside will be decorating for Christmas before the waitress makes her way through this crowd," Trevor said, sliding out of the banquette. "Regular? Decaf? Double espresso?"

"Cappucino," Jen told him. "Thanks."

A short, fat guy with a gray ponytail went to the mike. "Okay, once again, that was Michelle Nussbaum. Michelle asked me to tell you that she's got tapes of her original tunes for sale; meet her by the blue Jeep on Ocean, parked in front of the dry cleaners." He checked his clipboard. "Our next singer is from Boston. He sent a tape in to the New Voices contest at WGLB and is waiting to hear. Please welcome Darrian Darvey."

Now that Michelle and her entourage had left, there were only half as many people sitting near the stage. They applauded half-heartedly as Darrian climbed onstage and began ostentatiously to tune his guitar.

"Like he couldn't do that before he went up there," the girl sitting at the next table groused.

Jen laughed. "Not too pretentious, huh?"

"So beautiful and yet so alone," a familiar voice said dramatically.

Jen looked up to see Pacey, posed with his hand over his heart. "I could weep, Jen. I really could."

"Save it, Witter. I'm on a date," Jen said. Andie was standing near him. Andie looked to the right and to the left.

"With—?"

"Trevor. He went to get coffee. You guys want to squeeze in?" Jen offered.

"If there's room for more," Andie said, just as Dawson and Sarah joined them.

"Hey, Jen," Dawson said. "You here alone?"

"With Trevor." She turned to the girl sitting at the next table. "You mind if my friends squeeze in here?"

"Squeeze away," she said, and the four of them found room.

"So. You're with Trevor," Andie said brightly.

"That's what I said," Jen replied.

Andie nodded. "That's nice." She looked over at Pacey. "I assume you didn't leave your charges alone?"

"Oh, Casper's got the group under control," answered Pacey.

"We found someone to cover for us," corrected Dawson.

"Terrific, a party!" Trevor exclaimed as he deftly weaved his way over to them and handed Jen her drink.

"How goes it, Trevor?" Pacey asked. Even though Trevor had displayed a sliver of soul in dealing with Tia at the auditions, Pacey still didn't trust the guy.

Trevor found room next to Jen. "Wonderfully, actually." He wrapped his arm around Jen's shoulder.

"You have no idea how getting the lead in the play has changed Tia's life," Sarah told Jen. "It doesn't even bother her anymore when Britney and company rag on her. She counts the minutes every day until play practice."

"Walter too," Dawson said. "He's gone from belligerent white boy from the 'urbs who intimidates with his size, to Master Thespian."

"I think that's great," Trevor said.

Jen turned to him. "You'll see for yourself when you start playing for our rehearsals next week. They're really cute together."

Trevor gazed into Jen's eyes. "Are they?"

She studied his lips . . . and wondered what it would be like to kiss them. "Yeah. They are."

"Sing it with me, people!" Darrian yelled into the microphone.

Love ain't hate, hate's gotta wait,
Love ain't hate, hate's gotta wait . . .

Dawson winced. "Why would someone with such a tenuous grasp on pitch become a singer?"

Andie sighed. "You might as well ask me why someone with a newly strong dislike for seven-year-olds is spending the summer taking care of them."

"You didn't know you were going to get stuck on

pottie patrol," Sarah reminded her. "Hey, anyone up for darts?"

"Careful now," Pacey cautioned. "It's a little known fact that I happen to be the darts champion of Capeside."

"Since when?" Andie asked him.

Pacey fixed her with a mysterious look. "There is much you do not know about the great and powerful Pacey Witter, McPhee."

"Actually, I can't recall ever seeing you play a game of darts in your life," Andie said.

Pacey threw his hands into the air. "Fine. Clearly my mastery is being questioned. I shall have to prove myself to the doubters." He turned to Jen and Trevor. "You two coming?"

Jen regarded Trevor from under her eyelashes. "I think . . . not." Trevor's smile told her he appreciated her response.

"You heard the lady," he said.

"I believe they did," Jen said, her eyes still glued to Trevor. She didn't even notice when her friends walked away.

"So, Miss Lindley," Trevor began, "alone at last."

"If you call a hundred or so people and one bad singer alone."

"Figuratively speaking." His hand slid sensuously around her neck. "Do you have any idea how beautiful you are?"

"I'm assuming that's rhetorical."

Trevor threw his head back and laughed. "It's very rare to find a girl who is beautiful as well as funny, you know. Most intriguing."

Jen cocked her head at him. "What brought you to Camp Takabec, anyway?"

"It certainly wasn't a search for fame and fortune, was it," he said wryly. "Actually, I did my senior year as an exchange student in Boston, and my visa's not up until the fall."

"So you decided to spend your last few months in the United States at summer camp?" Jen asked dubiously.

"Call me crazy. I've always loved camp ever since I was a tyke. And the Tackman offered me quite a substantial bonus if I finish out the summer. After which, I'll still have six weeks to travel the country, with some money in my pocket."

"How very reasonable and mature of you."

"Did you take me for the unreasonable, immature sort, then?"

"Basically, yes," Jen admitted. "But then, I've been known to display those qualities myself on occasion."

"Really?" He used his index finger to gently trace the curve of her cheek. "Are you going to give me examples or is it irrelevant?"

Jen thought for a moment. "Well, let's see. You're going to disappear from my life in just a few weeks, and I'm going to disappear from yours. Which would seem to make this more of a 'live for the moment' kind of encounter."

"Good or bad?"

Jen shrugged. "It is what it is."

He cupped his fingers around the back of her neck, bringing her closer to him. "And what is it, Jen?"

Words were unnecessary. Their sizzling kiss told each other everything either of them needed to know.

Chapter 9

Ten cents, twenty cents, fifty, a dollar
All for the Lions, stand up and holler!
Go-o-o-o-o Lions!!

Gigi and her cheerleaders jumped into the air, shaking their green pom-poms lustily. It was the next morning, and Dawson was in a foul mood. The Bears were, once again, playing baseball against the Lions, their main camp nemesis. It was the ninth inning, and the score was eight to nothing. In fact, the Bears had only scored on the Lions in one game so far this summer, and that only happened because four of the Lions best players had been in the infirmary with poison ivy. Even that game they'd lost, 6–2.

As usual, Gigi and her cheerleaders were rooting for whichever team was playing against the Bears.

When Dawson had pointed out the patent unfairness of this to Mr. Tacky, as well as the anomaly of having cheerleaders at a baseball game, the camp director had told him that the Bears should think of it as incentive to get their game together, because no one wanted to cheer for losers.

Dawson rubbed the place between his eyes, where a headache was forming. Last night at the Coffee Café, Sarah had made it more than clear that she was interested in him. But though he liked her, the spark just wasn't there. He could tell it hurt her feelings, which was the last thing he wanted to do. On the other hand, he reasoned, it would be much worse to get involved with her if his feelings for her were really platonic.

He thought again to how he'd felt when they'd finished the dart game and gone back to their table to find Trevor and Jen in a passionate lip-lock. It clearly wasn't the first, either. In fact, shortly after that, Trevor and Jen excused themselves and went off together, to who-knew-where to do who-knew-what.

"Go get 'em, Caesar!" Pacey called to the kid who had just walked up to the plate. "Swing it nice and easy."

At home plate, Caesar leaned his bat against his legs, took a tiny bottle of antibacterial liquid cleanser out of the pocket of his shorts, and calmly washed his hands while the Lions razzed him.

"How obsessive-compulsive is that kid?" Pacey groaned to Dawson. "He sees germs everywhere."

"There are germs everywhere," Dawson replied.

"Thanks. Very helpful."

"Strike one," Jack, who was umpiring the game, called loudly as the first pitch crossed the plate.

Pacey cupped his hands to his mouth. "That's okay, kiddo, keep your eye on the—"

"Strike two!" Jack called.

"Oh, man," Kenny groaned from the Bears' bench, "we suck."

"Send Smelly out there and he can stink-bomb the Lions out of the game with his breath," Alan suggested. Smelly retorted by breathing hard right in Alan's face.

"Gross! Get me a fumigator!" Alan yelled.

"Cut it out, you guys," Dawson told them as the pitcher wound and delivered.

"Strike three!" Jack called. The Lions razzed the kid as Caesar slunk back to the Bears' bench.

"Walter's up. Andrew, you're on deck," Pacey told them.

"Hey, Fatboy! Go have another doughnut!" one of the Lions yelled to Walter.

"Shut up, fool," Walter mumbled, squaring his bulk behind the plate.

The Lions called a time-out—something having to do with their third baseman. Out of the corner of his eye, Dawson saw Mr. Tack and his sycophantic nephew, Pete, strolling over to the field. Great. Just what he needed, the Tackman to witness yet another humiliating defeat of his bunk. And right behind them, Dawson saw a large group of kids, boys and girls, heading up the path from free swim. They all stopped to watch the end of the game.

"Yo, in this lifetime?" Pacey called to the Lions' coach, Carl Brillstein.

544

"Don't get a hair up your butt," Carl called back. "My third baseman has a problem."

"Hey, ump," Pacey said to Jack. "You gonna allow this? Let's get this game underway."

"Much as I feel for your team, Pacey," Jack said, "all this time-out is doing is postponing the inevitable, so in the scheme of things, it hardly matters."

"He's right," Dawson told Pacey.

"Yeah." Pacey shook his head. "How is it that Mr. Tacky put every weird kid in the same bunk? And, more important, why can't we have at least one kid who can hit a baseball?"

"Who knows," Dawson replied. He noticed Trevor heading toward the dining hall with one of the younger, cuter nurses.

"There's something about that guy," Dawson said darkly.

"He's a player," Pacey said.

"And he's playing with Jen," Dawson noted.

"She's a big girl, Dawson. She can take care of herself."

"Okay, let's play ball!" Jack called as Carl jogged off the field.

Walter swung late at a fastball and ripped the ball down the first base line, where it skittered into the outfield for a hit. Then Andrew came up to bat with a chance to tie the game, but slapped the ball weakly into the outfield, where the right fielder caught the pop-up. Then, he fired the ball to first base, doubling Walter off the bag. A double play! It ended the game. The cheerleaders gave a final victory cheer, and the

Lions players all fist-bumped one another, as the Bears dragged back to their bench.

"All you guys need to ask yourselves is, 'Did I try my hardest?' " Pacey told them. "If the answer is 'Yes,' then you have nothing to feel badly about."

"Wanna bet?" Caesar asked.

"At least we got a hit," Smelly pointed out.

"Shut up, Smelly," Kenny told him. "It wasn't yours. You haven't gotten a hit all summer."

"Neither have you," Smelly retorted. "Once you got walked, but that was only because—"

"Bears? Pacey. Dawson."

Mr. Tack stood over the bedraggled group, his fingers laced behind his back.

"We were just about to take the guys down to the waterfront to swim," Pacey told the camp director.

"Not so fast," Mr. Tack said. He smiled grimly. His eyes scanned the Bears. "Quite the performance you boys just put on just now." The Bears hung their heads. No one said a word.

"Look, Mr. Tack," Dawson began, his voice low, "the Lions are still on the other side of the field. The cheerleaders are over there, and a lot of other kids are watching. I would really appreciate it if you said whatever it is you feel you have to say to these kids in private. Can you come back to the bunk with us?"

"Your unsolicited opinion is duly noted," Mr. Tack said. He eyed the Bears again. "Boys, do you realize that you are the laughingstock of my camp?" No one answered, because the answer was obvious.

"I don't like losers," the camp director continued. "There is only one way to change a loser to a winner.

You have to hit bottom and have that bottom make you feel so low that you'll do anything to crawl out of it. I'm doing this for your own good. Hit the field, boys." They all looked up at him, not comprehending.

"Hit the field, I said," the camp director repeated, and the campers reluctantly trudged out onto the infield.

"We'll start with fifty sit-ups," Mr. Tack announced. "On your backs, boys."

"I'm allergic to the dirt," Caesar objected.

"No, son, you're a hypochondriacal weenie," Mr. Tack said, his voice even. "Now, all of you, hit the dirt!" In full view of half the camp, the Bears lay down in dirt near second base and began to struggle through sit-ups.

"Five, six, seven . . ." Mr. Tack counted out loud. The campers watching joined in the count. Mr. Tack made no effort to stop them. "Ten, eleven, twelve!" they all yelled gleefully at the struggling Bears.

"This sucks," Pacey told Dawson as they stood on the third-base line, watching their campers be humiliated.

"I'd love to stop him, but short of putting my fist through his face, I can't think of a way to do that," Dawson said.

"Sixteen, seventeen, eighteen . . ."

Walter was struggling. He could barely lift his hefty upper body. "Come on, Chubby, work off that lard!" Mr. Tack yelled at him, red-faced.

Andrew started to wheeze. He stopped long enough to pull his ever-present inhaler of his pocket.

"Quit faking it, Casparian!" The Tackman boomed at him. "Get back to it!"

"Casper, Casper, Casper!" some kids began to chant. And even though it was against camp regulations for one camper to call another camper by a nickname, once again Mr. Takermann made no effort to stop the chanting.

Dawson couldn't take anymore. "Mr. Tack, Andrew is not faking it. He has very serious asthma and—"

"I'm the director and owner of this camp, Mr. Leery," Mr. Tack snapped. "I'm not unfamiliar with his medical records."

"Thirty-one, thirty-two, thirty-three . . ." The chanting from both cheerleaders and campers continued as the Bears struggled with their sit-ups. Dawson and Pacey exchanged looks.

"You thinking what I'm thinking?" Pacey asked Dawson.

"Yup," Dawson said. "It's a movie moment, but in this case, I think it's justified."

"Then let's do it," Pacey said, his jaw set tight.

By unspoken agreement, the two counselors trotted out onto the field, dropped to the ground, and joined the Bears in their sit-ups as the campers on the sidelines went wild with laughter. But the grateful glances from their humiliated bunk made it worth it. At least they were all in it together.

Only Caesar and Jason made it through all fifty sit-ups. The rest of the Bears lay prostate on the field. "On your feet, boys!" Mr. Tack yelled to the Bears. The campers struggled up from the dirt. Pacey and Dawson stood with them.

Mr. Tack marched over, Pete right behind him. "Boys, did you ever hear of General Patton?" Mr. Tack asked them. He launched into the biography of the famous general. Joey was just coming down the path from arts and crafts when she saw Dawson, Pacey, and their campers out on the field as Mr. Tack lectured them about General Patton, winners and losers. Meanwhile, the crowd of watching campers had gotten even larger as word spread quickly through camp of the Bears' in-progress public humiliation.

"What's up with that?" Joey asked Jack, coming up next to him.

"It seems Attila the Camp Director saw *Patton* one too many times. He has a thing about losers."

"General Patton did not put up with losers because he refused to associate with them!" Mr. Tack thundered, loud enough for Joey and Jack to hear. "Being a loser is a choice, boys. It's time to change your mindset!"

"What a cretin," Joey seethed. "He's the last person on earth who should be running a camp for kids. Look at that, Jack. The man is getting perverse pleasure from humiliating them."

"Repeat after me, boys," Mr. Tack instructed. "I can change from a loser to a winner!" The Bears shuffled around miserably and mumbled their response.

"You'll be out on this field until the end of camp if you don't say it like you mean it, boys," Mr. Tack threatened. "Now, let's hear it."

Pacey and Dawson fixed Mr. Tack with looks that

told him exactly what they thought of him as they yelled with their campers, "I can change from a loser to a winner!"

"Again!"

"I can change from a loser to a winner! I can change from a loser to a winner!"

"No you can't!" some camper on the sidelines yelled, which made everyone laugh hysterically. But Mr. Tack nodded.

"All right. The slate is wiped clean, Bears. This is the first day of the rest of your summer. Now, start acting like the winners I know you can be." He turned on his heel and headed for the dining hall, and the kids who had been watching the spectacle dispersed. Pacey and Dawson led their red-faced, miserable campers off the field, where they silently gathered up their equipment from the baseball game.

"He's loathsome," Joey told Dawson when she came over to join him and Pacey. "Beyond loathsome."

"I wholeheartedly agree," Dawson said wearily.

Jason came over to them. "The Tack is made to be bad personage."

"I agree," Dawson said.

"He make to feel not good the Bears," Jason continued. "In video I make him bad guy."

"Your English is really improving, Jason," Joey noted, which made the boy beam.

As Joey and Jason continued to talk, an idea began forming in Dawson's mind. It wasn't quitting his job in protest. That wouldn't help his bunk at all. Maybe Mr. Tack would become their counselor himself if that happened. But something Jason had said about the video he was making had just sparked another idea altogether. A way of bringing the Bears together and getting back at Mr. Tack at the same time.

"Guys, let's head back to our bunk," Dawson called. "We're about to confer in a top-secret meeting." The wheels turned in Dawson's head. His idea might just work.

"Dawson, what kind of scheme are you—" Joey began. She felt a hand on her back and turned around. It was Trevor.

"Hi there, lovely lady," he said. "Haven't seen you since our sail the other day. Fun, wasn't it?"

Joey nodded. She had to admit, it had been fun. Trevor had been great company, and he'd also been a perfect gentleman. "Want to do it again later?" Trevor asked.

"Sure," Joey agreed. "I'd like that."

As Dawson headed back to his bunk with his campers, he craned around to watch Trevor and Joey, laughing intimately together in what had been the Bears' dugout. He had a feeling that Joey was clueless as to the fact that Trevor and Jen had been in major make out mode the night before.

The question was, should he tell her or not?

Chapter 10

"Go, Dawson! Go, Dawson! Go, Dawson!" the Bears chanted gleefully.

"Hey, thanks for the support," Pacey said, feigning hurt feelings. "This is the finals of the Camp Takabec Dining Hall Sliding Plate Olympics, and I could have used your support."

Dawson and Pacey were sitting at opposite ends of the table, members of their bunk arrayed on both sides. Dawson eyed Pacey's plastic dessert plate, which hung precariously off the table in front of him. The idea was for Dawson to push his own plate down and get it even farther off the table on Pacey's end, without it actually falling off.

"I am ready," Dawson solemnly told his campers. With one gentle push on the plastic dessert plate, it slid down the length of the long wooden table.

"Too fast, man, you're gonna go overboard!" Kenny said. Wrong. The plate came to rest perfectly, with one half over the edge and one half on the table. "Dawson, you be man!" Jason cried, fist-bumping Walter.

"I believe what you're trying to say is, 'You da man,' Pacey corrected.

Jason nodded. "That what I be saying. Dawson, you da man."

"Nah," Dawson said, grinning at the kid, "*you* da man."

It had been ten days since Mr. Tacky had publicly humiliated the Bears, and he hadn't done anything like it since. Instead, his new approach was simply to pretend that the Bears didn't exist—a complete freeze-out, which, Dawson figured, was certainly preferable to overt and public humiliation.

At the head table, Pete, who sat next to Mr. Tack, stood up and blew shrilly on his whistle. Then Mr. Tack stood and cleared his throat. Alan eyed the loathed camp director. "I hope he announces that he's quitting."

"Or dying," Smelly added.

"Or both," Walter said. All around him, the Bears nodded their agreement.

"Okay, campers, listen up," Mr. Tack began. "I've got a few announcements about the terrific stuff we've got scheduled for your last week here at Takabec. The time really flew by, didn't it?"

"No," Andrew replied under his breath.

"First," Mr. Tack continued, "the night after next, in the time-honored tradition of Camp Homeric, is the annual girls-invite-the-guys Sadie Hawkins dance." There was a huge reaction to this—whoops, hollers, and groans. Walter turned to look at Tia, who sat at the next table.

"You kids," the camp director said fondly, as if he were their indulgent uncle. Then he waved his hands for quiet.

"What's the first rule of Camp Takabec?" Mr. Tack asked. "All for one and one for all, right? That means, guys, if a girl invites you to the dance, you don't turn her down unless you're too sick to drag yourself out of the infirmary."

A bunch of guy campers began to ostentatiously cough, holding their throats as if they were dying. Mr. Tack laughed and quieted them down again. "Alrighty, moving on. The next night is the camp musical *Grease*—I hear it's really super. Then—and I'm real excited about this, kids—it'll be the Girls versus Guys Camp Color War!"

Excited voices burst out anew as Pacey looked over at Dawson. "Ever hear of color war being girls against guys?"

"Just another wonderful innovation from the Tackman," Dawson replied.

"You'll compete in athletics, skits, songs, all kinds of fun stuff," the camp director said. "It'll be super. Then, on the last two nights of camp, the Bippie banquet—for all you kids who have been brave enough to jump into that water every morning—and the Final Banquet, when I will name the Best Bunk of the Twenty-first Century. So, Bippies, keep up the good work, and all of you, let's make the last few days of camp days to remember and cherish forever. That's it, now go to evening activities."

Pete jumped up and began a cheer. "Mr. Tack rocks! Mr. Tack rocks! Mr. Tack rocks!" Campers began to join in, until the chant was deafening. Only the Bears were silent.

"No way am I saying that," Caesar announced, folding his arms. All the other Bears nodded in agreement as they headed out of the dining room. Dawson noticed Trevor with Jen, laughing about something. She wrapped her arms around his neck.

"Question: What does she see in him?" Dawson asked Pacey.

"Maybe she's just using him for her carnal needs," Pacey suggested. "Wanton hussy. What're you up to tonight?"

"Miraculously enough, I'm off. But Jack asked me to meet him at the football field—the reason for this is evidently shrouded in mystery—so I'll be hanging around for a while. You?"

"Lifeguard duty for a sunset general swim. We still on for the bunk meeting at eight?"

"Absotively, my friend."

"See you then."

Dawson headed for the football field, where Jack had teed balls up at the twenty-, thirty-, and forty-yard lines and was kicking field goals, one after the other. Dawson watched, amazed, as his friend banged one right through the uprights from forty yards.

"Impressive," Dawson commented.

"Thanks."

"So Jack, why am I here?" Dawson asked. "And I don't mean in the existential sense."

"Actually . . . here comes your project now." Jack pointed toward the far end of the football field, where a small form in full football gear was chugging toward them.

"Dawson, meet Cassie," Jack introduced them. "Cassie, Dawson. Dawson's a bud of mine, and he's going to help us."

"Nice to meet you," the girl said. "I've seen you around camp. And thanks for the help."

"You're welcome, I think," Dawson said, slightly bemused. "To be perfectly frank, I have no idea what it is I'm helping with."

"Think of it as a Disney movie log line," Jack suggested. "Cassie's the only girl on the football squad. I've been doing some one-on-one, top-secret coaching with her. But what I really needed to work with her was another man. And you're it."

Dawson looked confused. "Since football is hardly my strong suit, why me?"

Jack grinned. "Because I knew you'd say yes. Let's go to the end zone."

Dozens of footballs littered the ground. "We're working on Cassie's pass-receiving skills. She needs a defensive back to cover her. Dawson, congratulations. You're a defensive back."

"But, Jack, she's small," Dawson objected. "I don't want to hurt her."

Cassie looked him in the eye. "You won't hurt me. And even if you do, I can take it." Jack smiled his approval at Cassie. She looked back at him with something close to reverence.

"Okay, Cassie, twenty-five zero, on two. Dawson, stick with her. Ready, one, two!"

The girl broke from the goal line and ran straight at Dawson, who backpedaled furiously. Then, she faked to the right and cut sharply to the left at the twenty-yard stripe. Jack led her perfectly with a pass, and Dawson could only make a futile effort to knock it down.

"Touchdown!" Cassie cried, her voice muffled by the helmet.

"Do it again," Jack told her sternly.

He went for a different play this time—a pure slant—but with the same result. The girl receiver beat Dawson, and Jack connected with the pass. And again. And again.

"Give me a white flag to wave," Dawson told Cassie. "I surrender. And to think I was worried about hurting you. When are you planning to turn pro?"

The girl looked at Jack. "If Jack will be my coach, I'll turn pro tomorrow."

"Hey, you're the one doing all the work out there," Jack told her. "I'm just the one throwing the passes."

"My coach is modest, huh?" Cassie told Dawson. "And he's also the best."

"I agree," Dawson told her. He looked at his watch. "I have a top-secret meeting I need to be at in five minutes, so I'll leave you two to your practice."

"Thanks for helping out," Cassie told him. Then she fired a football at his stomach, which he barely caught in time. "And no offense, Dawson, but you're not really much of a defensive back."

"No offense taken, I promise," Dawson told her as he took off toward his bunk.

"He's nice," Cassie told Jack.

"He's been a great friend to me. When my sister, Andie, and I moved to Capeside, it was . . . well, let's just say it isn't easy being the new kid in the small-town high school."

Cassie took off her helmet and raked her fingers through her messy hair. "I know it's still a couple of years away for me, but I think going to high school will be scary," she admitted.

"Hey, you're tough," Jack told her.

"But girls don't seem to like me very much. I have more guy friends. I don't mean in a boyfriend way," she hastily added, staring at the helmet in her hands. "To tell you the truth, I've never had an actual boyfriend."

"You're only twelve, Cassie. Give it time."

"I feel way older than twelve." She looked up at him. "Don't you think I act older? I mean, do you think of me as some little kid?"

"No."

"Age is just a number," Cassie said earnestly. She fixed her eyes on her helmet again. She cleared her throat. She kicked her cleats into the dirt. "So . . . um . . . I was wondering . . . if you would wanna go to the Sadie Hawkins dance with me."

Jack was so taken aback that for a moment he didn't say anything. "You can say no," Cassie went on quickly. "I mean, you don't have to feel obligated to say yes. Probably it was stupid for me to—"

"Cassie."

"What?" She risked looking up at him again, her face beet red with embarassment.

"I would be honored to go with you to the Sadie Hawkins dance," Jack said.

A smile lit up her face. "Really?"

"Really."

"Jack McPhee, this is the happiest day of my life."

Smelly fired a pillow at Caesar that hit him in the head. "Direct hit! I score!"

"Oh, great. I'm gonna have to wash my hair again because of that," Caesar protested.

"The pillow doesn't have germs, you weenie," Alan said.

"Are you kidding?" Caesar asked. "Pillows are a breeding ground for staph, strep—"

"Strep this!" Walter yelled, lobbing a small bean bag at Caesar's stomach.

"Yo, no bloodshed right before bedtime," Pacey told them.

"What's the matter, got a hot date?" Alan asked, leering at Pacey. "You don't want to get held up?"

"You got it, Alan," Pacey agreed. "With Charma." The Bears all groaned or held their noses or threw themselves on the floor pretending to have fits.

"Hey, what if she invites you to the Sadie Hawkins dance?" Kenny asked. "Then you'd have to be seen with her in public."

Andrew sat on the edge of Pacey's bed. "No one is going to ask me to the dance."

"So, who wants to go, anyway?" Smelly asked. "The girls here suck."

"That's kind of a broad statement, isn't it?" Pacey asked.

"So?" Smelly shrugged.

"Walter loves Britney," Caesar hooted. "He wants to feel her up!"

"Shut up, fool," Walter snapped.

"Yes, fool," Jason echoed.

Dawson walked in the door and all the Bears began to lob questions at him about the dance, girls, and how to get them.

"You guys think Dawson knows and I don't?" Pacey asked. "I happen to be a chick magnet."

"I suggest we table the chick magnet conversation and bring this top-secret meeting to order," Dawson suggested. "How is our project coming?"

"It bad," Jason assured him.

"He means good," Caesar translated, rolling his eyes. "He's trying to talk like Walter."

Jason nodded. "Me and posse be film fools. We chill."

"Good to see the Ebonics project is going well," Pacey quipped.

"Jason, I don't think that's the kind of English your relatives in Slovakia wanted you to learn during your summer in America."

"What be Ebonics?" Jason asked.

"Let's move on," Dawson decided. "Do we give Tack forty-eight hours to mend his ways before we launch Operation Get Even? Andrew?"

"I've fed all the data about the Tackmeister into

the personality profiler program on my computer. There's a ninety-one percent chance that as the end of camp approaches, it's only going to get worse, not better."

"Come on, Dawson, you know the dude ain't gonna mend his ways," Walter said. "Far as I'm concerned, he be toast."

"Toast," Jason agreed. Dawson and Pacey exchanged looks.

"Okay, then," Pacey said. "It's a deal. Hands in."

As they had been doing every night for the last couple of weeks, the Bears put their hands together, like a basketball team before the opening tip-off of a game. "We are the Bears," Pacey said. "And we know what Bears eat for breakfast, right?"

"Tacks!" the Bears chortled then they all fist-bumped one another enthusiastically. Soon enough, it would be payback time.

Pacey and Dawson headed for the art and crafts cabin. They'd made a let's-get-the-hell-out-of-camp date with Joey, Jen, and Andie to spend the evening watching movies at Dawson's. At the moment, there were no guests at Potter's, which gave Joey some rare free time.

"How's the play coming?" Dawson asked Pacey.

"In my highly biased opinion, Tia and Walter leave Travolta and Olivia Newton-John in the dust. It behooves me to add, however, that they are only ten years old, playing at stuff they haven't experienced yet."

Pacey snapped his fingers. "That reminds me, I

forgot to give Tia the note about—" He reached into his back pocket for his script, but it was gone.

"I must have left my script down at the water-front," he told Dawson. "I've got all my genius-level directing notes in it so I gotta go find it. I'll meet you and the others at your house," he added, taking off toward the waterfront.

It was kind of peaceful, Dawson thought, walking alone in the steamy night air, with only the crickets for company. Camp was usually so noisy. It was amazing that the time had gone by so quickly. In one way, he resented having used up so much of his summer being a camp counselor. The only film work he'd done in the past month was with the kids in film club. On the other hand, though, as weird as the Bears were, Dawson really liked them. And he truly thought he and Pacey had made a difference in their lives.

Or, that could just be sentimental crap.

He went right at the fork that led to the arts and crafts cabin. He was a little early, he knew, so he figured he'd just hang and wait for Joey. But as he got closer, he noticed two figures in front of the cabin. It wasn't until he was almost on top of them that Dawson realized it was Joey and Trevor. They seemed to be so involved with each other that they hadn't even heard him.

Dawson ostentatiously cleared his throat, and they broke apart.

"Oh, hi," Joey said self-consciously, pushing some hair behind her ear. "Um. You're early."

"Evidently," Dawson replied.

"Gorgeous night, isn't it?" Trevor asked, perfectly at ease. His arm snaked around Joey's waist.

"Pretty garden variety, actually," Dawson replied tersely. "You ready to go, Joey?"

"Sure. Just . . . give me a minute." Dawson stood there.

"That was her ever so polite way of saying you should shove off for a few," Trevor explained.

"What is your problem?" Dawson asked Trevor.

"Haven't got one."

"Okay, then, I have a problem. With you," Dawson said.

"Hold on," Joey broke in. "Whatever it is you think you're doing, Dawson, is totally out of line and unacceptable. Why don't you just go and I'll meet you at your house."

"Joey, I think you need to understand that this guy—"

"I mean it, Dawson," Joey insisted, eyes blazing.

Dawson turned to Trevor. "Please consider what I'm about to say a threat. Do not, I repeat do *not*, play games with people I care about. Because I will make you very sorry."

"I've no idea what you're talking about, mate."

"Just go, Dawson," Joey pleaded. "Shut up and go."

Dawson threw his hands in the air and turned on his heel. First Jen. Now Joey. Who knew how many other girls at camp Trevor was dogging? To tell or not to tell, Dawson mused darkly as he headed toward the main gate of the camp.

That is most definitely the question.

*   *   *

Pacey was sure he'd had his script in his back pocket when he'd gone to lead the sunset swim. Jen had hung out for a while, and he'd kept one eye on the swimmers while he went over his notes with her. So the script had to be there somewhere.

The full moon was bright enough to illuminate the entire dock, but Pacey didn't see his *Grease* script anywhere. And he really, really needed those notes.

Where else could it be? He'd put his towel on the hooks at the main lifeguard stand, so maybe he'd left his script there. He and Jen were constantly ragging on the kids for forgetting their scripts, so he couldn't very well admit that he'd lost his. He headed for the lifeguard stand.

Unclaimed towels. One swim fin. Half of a sandwich. But no—

Wait, what was that sticking out of the lost-and-found box? Yes! His script. It had to have been someone's idea of a joke, to put his script in there instead of returning it to him. After all, his name was on the cover in letters.

"Well, if it isn't Mister Director," a female voice purred.

Pacey looked around. Who had said that, and where was she?

"Over here, Pacey." The soft sound of water slapping made Pacey peer out into the bay. Someone was definitely out there swimming.

"I can't see who you are," Pacey told her.

"And here I thought you'd recognize my voice, silly boy," the girl said. "It's Gigi."

Gigi. Ouch. He detested Gigi. "Hi," Pacey called back to her. "Have a great swim. See ya."

"Wait a sec," she called to him. "Could you come over here? There's something important I need to tell you, Pacey. And I really don't want to have to scream it to you."

Reluctantly, Pacey went out to the end of the dock. Now he could see her red hair, slicked back by the water, glinting in the moonlight. "What's up?" he asked her.

"Come a little closer," she suggested.

He knelt down near the edge of the dock.

"Did you know that if a girl gives up all dairy foods, white flour, and sugar, counts her calories religiously, and works out on a regular basis, she ends up with an unbelievable body?"

"I'm more than willing to take your word for that, Gigi."

She flung something at him that hit him in the face.

It was the top of her bikini.

"I thought you might like to check it out for yourself," she offered. "Up close. And very personal."

Pacey paused. Okay. A gorgeous girl swimming topless had just basically offered to act out a bootleg Pamela Lee video with him. He was frankly getting a little tired of his much-abused and highly graphic fantasy life, but he really, truly, deeply did not like this girl.

At the moment, he rued the day he had developed scruples. Life was so much easier for slacker Pacey than the newer, supposedly improved model. He leaned over closer to her and thought fast.

"That is a generous offer," he told her. "But I have this girlfriend—agh!"

With a flash of incredible breasts, she had bounced half out of the water, grabbed his T-shirt, and toppled him over into the water.

And then she proved that she was fully qualified to give him mouth-to-mouth.

Chapter 11

"And that's the whole tawdry tale," Pacey concluded. He was sitting on the floor of Dawson's room, leaning against the bed. Jen was next to him, and Dawson was sitting on the foot of his bed. Pacey had just finished explaining why he had had to go back to his bunk and change his dripping wet clothes before he could come meet them.

Jen shot him an incredulous look. "You're telling us that Gigi tried to seduce you?"

"Why does your tone of voice imply such astonishment, Lindley?" Pacey asked, reaching for a slice of pizza from the box in front of him.

"Because Gigi has no taste," Jen replied.

Pacey grinned. "Good answer." He took a big bite of the now cold pizza, which didn't bother him after several days of camp food. "Also, let me remind you that I said she *tried* to seduce me. I didn't say she succeeded."

Dawson laughed his disbelief.

"You're telling us Gigi threw her bathing suit top at you, then pulled you into the water with her," Jen said, "and Pacey 'Horny Toad' Witter turned her down?"

Pacey put his hands over his heart. "Oh, ye of little faith. Anyway, what happened to Joey and Andie?"

"Joey took Andie with her to make a pit stop at home before heading over here," Dawson explained. "According to Joey, both Bessie and Alexander have come down with the flu, so she stayed to help. Andie-to-the-rescue stayed with her."

"Just as well," Pacey said, polishing off his slice. "It would have felt monumentally strange to tell that story in front of her."

"The original point of this unexpected sexual ambush was to find your lost *Grease* script," Dawson reminded him. "Did you?"

"Affirmative. And I'm telling you, Gigi's sexual ambush was not successful. Not that I'm loathe to indulge in empty and meaningless sex with a girl who aspires to become a Dallas Cowboys cheerleader. But I had this sick feeling in the pit of my stomach, Dawson, when I realized that your annoying sense of honor appears to be rubbing off on me."

"I'll take that as a twisted compliment," Dawson replied. He reached for the video boxes on his dresser. "For tonight's viewing pleasure you have your choice of *Papillon* or *One Flew Over the Cuckoo's Nest*. Somehow working for Tacky led me to choose classic tales of psychological survival in an oppressive institution."

"Actually, Dawson, I took the liberty of picking out a film for us," Jen told him as she reached for her backpack. "Something a bit more plebeian."

"Please don't tell me you went for *The Bad News Bears*."

"I didn't." Jen held up the video for the guys to see.

"*Grease*?" Dawson groaned.

Pacey gave her a thumbs-up. "Good idea."

"It's musical diabetes," Dawson complained.

"It's research," Jen insisted. "Two against one, Dawson. Sorry, we're watching *Grease*." She popped the cassette into Dawson's cassette player.

"I demand arbitration," Dawson said. "This was supposed to be a non–camp-related evening."

Jen scrambled onto the bed next to him and playfully nudged his shoulder. "Come on, Dawson, cheer up. Next time you rent something incomprehensible with subtitles I promise to sit through the whole thing without falling asleep."

"I'm holding you to that," Dawson warned, examining the cover of the *Grease* video box. "Did I mention how much I loathe the music in this treacly ode to comic teendom?"

"Multiple times," Pacey assured him.

"I'm kinda getting to like it," Jen said as the pre-movie trailers played on the TV. "Maybe it's because Trevor plays them so well. The man is a genius with his hands."

Oh, swell, Dawson thought. *When I leave camp, Joey is practically kissing the guy, and when I get*

132

here, Jen is lusting after the guy. And if I tell either one of them about it, they will both tell me to mind my own business. Why do they always shoot the messenger, anyway?

Jen checked her watch. "You're in luck, Dawson. I won't be able to stay for the whole movie. I'm meeting Trevor in forty-five minutes at the Coffee Café."

"Don't you find him just slightly shallow?" Dawson asked.

"To tell you the truth, Dawson, it wasn't depth I was looking for."

"Camp curfew is in an hour and a half," Dawson reminded her.

"So?" Jen replied. "It's good to live dangerously."

"At times," Dawson agreed. "But have you noticed how Trevor sniffs out anything with future child-bearing ability? Don't you find that rather demeaning?"

"Tell you what, Dawson," Jen said. "If he proposes to me tonight, I won't marry him. How's that?"

When Dawson's face remained grave, she hit the Pause button on the VCR. "Look, Dawson. It's just a summer thing. Like the one you could have had with Sarah but decided not to have, and undoubtedly would have been much happier having had."

"Would you have the same laissez-faire attitude if Trevor was having simultaneous 'summer things' with other girls?" Dawson asked.

"Is that a hypothetical?"

"I don't know, Jen. Is it?"

"Time out, you two," Pacey called, phone in hand. "While you two were arguing, I called Joey to see how they're doing over there, and she wants to talk to you, Dawson." He handed Dawson the phone.

"Joe?"

"Hi," Joey said. "Bessie and Alexander finally got to sleep and Andie headed back to camp." There was a long pause. "Look, Dawson, about you walking up on me and Trevor—"

"Where you choose to put your lips these days is none of my business," Dawson told her. "You've made that abundantly clear."

"I didn't mean to be so . . . whatever I was," Joey said. "It's just that it's still weird to have you see me with other guys. And I guess I overreacted. I apologize."

"Accepted," Dawson said.

"Trevor was so great about it," Joey continued. "I explained that we used to be . . . that we're still . . . whatever it is we are, and he said he totally understood."

Trevor again. Did the guy have some kind of bizarre power over women?

"He's a prince among men," Dawson said sourly.

"I think you ought to know, Dawson, that I've invited him to the Sadie Hawkins dance and he's accepted. I just don't want it to come as a surprise to you. I understand that even though you know it's inappropriate, your visceral reaction to seeing me with another guy is still jealousy, but—"

"Joey, I am not jealous."

"Fine. Don't admit it."

Dawson's hand tightened on the phone. "Gotta go, Joey. Jen rented *Grease*. Sandy's about to tell her friends the meaningful story of how she fell for Danny over the summer. You know how much that means to me." He hung up.

Jen and Pacey looked at him questioningly. "Trust me, it doesn't bear repeating," Dawson said wearily. He reached for the now empty pizza box and threw it Frisbee-style into his wastebasket. "Sorry, Jen, but I'm just not up for watching a teen parody of love tonight. I promise to applaud my heart out for your version of it on the stage, though."

Jen kissed him on the cheek. "Joey tell you something that bummed you out?"

"You might say that."

"Here's a concept, Dawson," Pacey said, clapping him on the back. "It may not be too late to catch Gigi at the waterfront. Me, you, doesn't matter. I don't think 'discerning' is her middle name. And you definitely need more tawdry lust in your life."

"My interest in Gigi is in the negative numbers." Dawson turned to Jen. "Question. I am utterly stymied about something that I would truly like to understand. What is it that women really want?"

Jen laughed too hard to manage an answer.

Trevor's kisses were making Jen dizzy. If they hadn't been snuggled into a dimly lit corner of the Coffee Café, she would have felt self-conscious about the overt P.D.A.

"You are a sizzling woman, Jen Lindley," Trevor told her, his lips against her neck. "How did I get so lucky?"

Jen smiled. "A question I've been asking myself.

When I lived in New York, all the English guys my friends and I ever met were total dogs to women."

"You see," Trevor teased her. "Never judge an English footballer—you'd call them soccer players—by his reputation."

"They also had reps as being too hot to resist."

"And do I qualify?"

"I'm considering it," Jen admitted.

"Well, then, I will remain hopeful." He took a sip of his coffee, his eyes still on hers. "I would really like to be alone with you, Jen."

"I'd like that too."

"Somehow macking it up in a café seems rather ludicrous." He reached for her hand. "But as you know Capeside and I don't, where might we go for privacy?"

"Definitely not my house. I live with my grand-mother."

Jen checked her watch. Twelve-thirty, meaning counselor curfew had come and gone a half-hour ago. On the other hand, it wasn't like there was a staff bed check. And Charma was one of the sound-est sleepers she'd ever seen.

"I'm afraid the best I can suggest is a walk in the park," Jen told Trevor.

He smiled at her. "You're on."

The park was only a few blocks from the café, and it was a balmy night. The scent of the ocean was in the air. "What a glorious place this is," Trevor said as they strolled hand in hand.

"I'd pretty much concur with that opinion," Jen said. "Although sometimes the small-town thing feels like a noose around my neck. Most of the time, though, I love it here."

When they reached the park, Trevor led Jen to a bench under a giant elm tree. He took her into his arms and kissed her until her IQ slumped.

"Whoa, time out," she said breathlessly, pulling away from him. "This is not a bedroom."

"Funny how kissing you makes me forget that." He reached for her again.

"Slow down, Romeo. I think we need to cool down a few degrees."

"Crushing," Trevor said. "I guess this means you only want me for my mind."

"Busted," Jen said, laughing. She really did like him. "I'd like to pose your mind a question, actually."

"Pose away."

"Would you like to go to the Sadie Hawkins dance with me?"

"Now, that's a tough one," Trevor mused, scratching his chin. "Five female counselors, one nurse, and assorted pre-pubescent campers have already requested the pleasure of my company."

"Aren't you the popular one. This means I'll have to go with my second choice. Walter."

Trevor laughed. "The ten-year-old Ebonics-speaking, two-hundred-pound Danny Zuko. How can I compete with that? I suppose I'll just have to turn all those other girls down and say yes to you."

"Excellent decision." She wrapped her arms around his neck. "Now, where were we?"

*   *   *

Jen yawned sleepily as she pushed her feet into her athletic shoes. She hadn't gotten back to camp until around three in the morning, which meant she'd only had about four and a half hours of sleep. Even the loud blasts of reveille hadn't awakened her, nor her campers, who were sleepily getting up and dressed. Charma had left a note saying she was down at the waterfront getting the day into gear.

It was nice of Charma to let me sleep, Jen thought, as she tried to stretch the kinks out of her back. Hours spent kissing on a park bench hadn't been the most comfortable thing in the world. Not that she'd realized it at the time.

Jen had just gotten dressed and found her script—they were doing a complete run-through of the play after breakfast—when Charma and Gigi entered the cabin.

"Good morning," Charma said briskly. "We need to talk."

" 'We' meaning the three of us?" Jen asked. "Did you and Gigi bond overnight or something?"

Charma ignored Jen's question. "Gigi said she saw you and another counselor in downtown Capeside last night past midnight curfew."

"Trevor Braithwaite," Gigi said smugly. "I saw the two of you walking into the park together."

"And just how could you have seen that, Gigi?" Jen asked, "unless you were out past curfew too?"

"You think you're so clever," Gigi sneered, with a patented flip of her red ponytail. "It just so happens that I had permission from Mr. Takermann to go to the late movie at the Rialto with my friend Belinda

McGovern. She lives in Capeside and she's been away all summer, so—"

"I know exactly who Belinda McGovern is," Jen interrupted. "Why does it not surprise me to learn you two are bosom buddies?"

"That is entirely beside the point," Gigi said, folding her arms. "Camp rules are camp rules, and you broke them."

"I was fast asleep by eleven," Charma told Jen, "so I had no idea what time you came in. Are her allegations true?"

"Yes."

Charma turned to Gigi. "Okay, you made your big report. You can go now. I need to talk to Jen alone."

"But—"

"Go work on your cartwheels or something," Jen advised.

"Fine," Gigi said smugly. "You can blame your friend Pacey for this, Jen. If he hadn't been so rude to me, maybe I would have let your indiscretion slide." She flounced off, her hair bouncing behind her.

"Okay, so let me make sure I've got the scenario straight," Charma barked. "You were out with a guy, it got late, you forgot what time it was."

"I didn't forget. I knew exactly what time it was."

"Deliberately flaunting the rules, eh? Very bad form. On the other hand, the only thing that I hate more than kids who leave their towels on the waterfront after general swim so that I have to pick them up and take them to the laundry bin is a tattletale. Frankly, Gigi annoys the hell out of me."

"Join the club," Jen said.

Charma strolled pensively to the other end of the cabin, then turned back to Jen. "Okay, here's what happened. You asked me if you could be out after curfew last night for some special reason—we'll figure that one out later. I said it was fine and that I'd clear it with Mr. Takermann, but telling him slipped my mind. The end."

Jen's jaw dropped. "Why would you do that for me?"

"I have no idea, because you don't deserve it," Charma replied. "You're lazy, self-indulgent, self-involved, and overprivileged."

"Now I don't even like me," Jen said.

"But you're honest. And you're great with kids. So I'm your cover for last night. Just don't let it happen again."

"I can't tell you how much I appreciate it," Jen said. "But I certainly don't want you to take the blame for what I did."

"Believe me, Mr. Tacky needs me much more than I need him. I'll talk to Gigi. Once she hears that I'm backing you up, I doubt that she'll tell him at all."

"Thanks, Charma. I owe you."

"You're right, you do. So make sure none of your campers leave their towels on the waterfront ever again."

"Got one! I got one! Holy-moley, I got one!" Smelly started reeling furiously as Dawson and all the Bears dropped their fishing rods and ran over to him. Pacey was at the playhouse for a final rehearsal of the play, but Andie and her seven-year-olds were fishing on the docks too, and they did the same thing. Within a few seconds, the boy was ringed by a double semicircle, girls in front, boys in the back.

Capeside Bay was brackish, and it supposedly held both freshwater and saltwater species. But the largest fish to come out of it during the entire summer had been an ugly sculpin that weighed less than a half pound. This evening's fishing event was scheduled to try once again to break that record.

"Don'chu be losin' fish!" Jason cried in broken Ebonics.

Lillith asked Andie, "What language was that?"

Smelly's rod was bent over nearly double as the boy struggled with whatever he'd hooked. Dawson edged his way in through the semicircle so he could stand by the boy's side. "Take it easy," he advised. "You've got him hooked, now just wear him out."

"Those skills we learned in boot camp sure came in handy, huh," Andie said.

"And I rented *A River Runs Through It* the other night as a refresher course," Dawson responded with a grin.

"Everything you ever needed to know you learned from film," Andie quipped. "Hang in there, big guy," she added to the struggling camper.

"Go, Smelly!" Alan cheered.

"Too heavy!" he grunted. "This is a big one."

Lillith started to cry. "He's hurting the fish!"

"No he's not," Andrew reassured her. "Fish have very little development in their nervous system. The fish at the other end of Smelly's line doesn't feel any pain."

"Are you sure?"

"Completely," Andrew said.

Dawson continued coaching the boy as the fish neared the surface. The water boiled as it tried to turn tail when it saw the dock. But Melvin kept the pressure on, and Dawson grabbed the net and swung it under the fish.

"Yeah!" Smelly cheered as his fish came out of the water. "It's a whopper!" The Bears all offered their congratulations as Walter beamed with pride.

"Technically, it's a bluefish," Dawson said. "So whatever you do, don't put your fingers in his mouth. He bites. You know the rule, Melvin—"

"We eat what we catch," the boy recited dutifully.

Dawson nodded. "I bet he's four pounds."

"Let's take him to the nature lodge," Andrew suggested. "We can take some pictures of him." Everyone thought this was a great idea, so the whole group trooped off to the nature lodge, just up the dirt road from the docks. Smelly carried the net that held his fish. Once at the lodge, the campers crowded inside, leaving Dawson and Andie alone on the deck.

"You've worked a miracle with those boys," Andie told him.

"Pacey and I really like them. You would too, if you got to know them."

"Frankly, since I teetered on geekdom myself at that age, the idea of counseling a bunk full of them is less than appealing."

"Come on, Andie. You were never a geek."

"Picture a junior Tracy Flick from *Election*," Andie said dryly. "That was me."

"Well, then, it appears you've outgrown it."

"How gallant of you to say so, Dawson. In fact, I would say that gallantry is one of your many good qualities."

"To what do I owe these compliments?"

Andie shrugged. "Merely voicing my thoughts." She cleared her throat nervously. "Which actually leads me to a question I've been meaning to ask you."

"Shoot."

"You can say no," Andie warned. "I won't be crushed or anything. And I don't mean this in a way that you might take this, so I want you to know that—"

"Andie, stop," Dawson said. "You're adding caveats to something you haven't even asked me yet."

"True. Okay, then, here it is. Dawson, would you go to the Sadie Hawkins dance with me?"

Chapter 12

Dressed in a floral summer dress, her hair half-piled on her head, Joey sat on the edge of Trevor's bed in the infirmary and held his hand. "You look so lovely, Joey," he told her. "I'm devastated not to be able to go to the dance with you."

"It's not your fault if you got sick." She felt his forehead, which was perfectly cool.

"I took three aspirins an hour ago," Trevor explained. "Sweated out the fever. If only I didn't feel so weak."

"Listen, I wouldn't let you get out of bed even if you tried to," Joey told him. "You might be contagious. The last thing we need is a camp full of sick kids."

Trevor nodded. "Thanks for being so understanding. Do go to the dance, though. I'd hate to think I ruined your evening."

Joey smiled. "Actually, I have someone in mind as my escort. I have reason to believe there's a chance he's still available." Joey left the infirmary and quickly walked the pathway toward the Bears' bunk. The Sadie Hawkins dance was starting in a half-hour. She just hoped she wasn't too late to snag her date. Before she even got to the door of the bunk, she heard the Bears at full volume.

"You can't make us go to some stupid dance!" one kid was saying.

"Everyone's gonna laugh at us!" another kid added, then lots of voices agreed.

Joey knocked on the door. Dawson swung it open. "Look, guys," he was saying at the same time, "you don't seem to understand that—"

He saw Joey. She was wearing a dress he'd never seen before. There were flowers in her hair.

"You're beautiful," he said softly.

"Ooh," the Bears cried in various tones of falsetto.

"Hey, do you guys do it?" Kenny asked eagerly. "You know, all the way? Home run?"

"Not a cool question to ask, Kenny," Pacey told him.

"Yeah, you be rude, man," Walter snapped. "Don't go askin' the man about his love life."

"How else am I supposed to learn?"

"What's up, Joey?" Dawson asked. "Where's your date?"

"The infirmary." She took in his chinos and button-down shirt, something she hadn't seen on him since camp started. "I guess you already have plans for the dance."

"Yes, I do. Believe me, if I hadn't already agreed to go with someone else I'd be happy to fill in for—"

"I wasn't asking you to," Joey said. "Is that what you thought?"

"Isn't that what you just implied?"

"Don't think so."

Joey stepped into the cabin. None of the Bears were dressed for the dance. They all had on their usual shorts and T-shirts, though Mr. Tack had decreed that the dance was a pants and button-down shirt affair.

"The Bears are boycotting the dance," Pacey told her.

"No girls invited any of us and no girl is gonna want to dance with any of us so why should we have to go just to stand around looking stupid?" Caesar asked. "Face it, we're losers."

Joey walked over to Andrew, who sat cross-legged on his bed, reading a Marvel comic book. "Andrew?"

He looked up at her. "Yes?"

"I was wondering if you would do me the honor of being my escort to the dance tonight?" Joey asked him.

Every eye in the bunk was on Andrew. Every jaw was on the floor. "I would like that very much," he said, dazed.

"Great," Joey told him. "You can pick me up at my bunk in a half-hour. See you then." Joey waved goodbye to the awestruck bunk as she walked out the door.

"Man, you have to tell me if she puts out!" she

heard Kenny bellow as she headed away, a giant smile on her face.

Jen sat on the edge of Trevor's bed in the infirmary. "I came by earlier but the nurse told me you were sound asleep and she really didn't want to wake you. I'm so sorry you're sick. Is there anything I can do?"

Trevor shook his head weakly. "I'm only sorry to miss going to the dance with you."

"That's hardly important," Jen assured him. "If I knew whatever you have wasn't catchy, I'd offer to stay and give you a back rub. For medicinal purposes only, of course."

"Your generosity is exceeded only by your good looks." He coughed. "Sorry. I'm just going to rest up as much as possible. I promise I'll be there to play the piano for *Grease* tomorrow night, even if I have to drag myself to the playhouse hooked up to an IV."

"Great. Well, I'll let you go back to sleep." She kissed her finger and put it to his lips. "'Til later."

As soon as Jen left the infirmary, Staci, the youngest of the nurses, tiptoed into the room. "She gone?"

"Like the wind," Trevor assured her, sitting up and putting his hands behind his head. "That should take care of both of my little dates for the evening."

"You shouldn't have said yes to both of them," Staci chided. "You're mighty lucky I was willing to pretend that you're sick, mister. Not to mention telling Jen you were asleep and couldn't be disturbed when Joey was in here."

"When you're right, you're right," Trevor agreed. "I

have a weakness for beautiful women. Speaking of which . . ." he held his muscular arms out to her. "Want to play doctor?"

Jen leaned against the wall, sipping some hideous punch concoction and looking over the dining hall, which had been transformed via tiny Christmas lights into the magical site of the Sadie Hawkins dance. Mr. Tacky was playing DJ. She watched the couples dancing: Dawson and Andie, Jack and that scrappy little girl, Cassie, who was on the football team. She certainly didn't look like a football player now. She had on a pastel skirt and a pink sweater, and she was looking at Jack as if he were the only boy in the world.

It was kind of amusing, actually, since Jack had secretly confessed to Jen a certain attraction—purely physical—to Trevor. *I guess we share the same taste in guys*, Jen thought wryly.

Pete Takermann came strolling in, with none other than Gigi on his arm. Gigi wore a semiformal and a wrist corsage. Pete looked as if he'd just won the lottery. Perfect couple.

Pacey hadn't mentioned if anyone had asked him to the dance, Jen realized. Maybe she could find him and they could go together, if only for—

Pacey walked into the dining hall holding ten-year-old Tia's hand. She had on platform shoes and lipstick, and she looked so serious and earnest that Jen wanted to hug her tightly.

Jen walked over to them. "Hi."

Tia blushed happily. "Pacey is my date."

"So I see. You make a lovely couple."

She blushed even harder. "Thanks."

Pacey turned and bowed to Tia. "May I have this dance?"

"Yes. You may." A ballad was playing. Pacey held Tia at a decorous arm's-length and danced her around the dance floor.

In a halter sundress, Britney danced by with Brad. "What happened, Tia?" she sneered, "all the Bears turn you down?"

Jen tapped Britney on her bare shoulder. "Oh, Britney?"

"What?"

"You have a massive green thing hanging out of your nose."

Britney gasped and shoved her pinky into her nostril as Jen wandered off. She waved to Sarah, who was dancing with a cute guy from culinary school who was spending the summer as the camp chef. Well, good for Sarah. Then she saw Dawson, with Andie in his arms. Well, well. What that meant, she had no idea.

As Jen went to throw out the rest of her punch, the Bears—washed, combed, and buttoned down—trouped into the dance en masse. They looked as if they were heading for a date with a firing squad.

"Hey, guys," Jen greeted them. "You look great." They remained stone-faced, and Jen realized one of the Bears was missing. "Where's Andrew?"

"Over there," Alan said, cocking his head to the door. Diminutive Andrew's pale, proud face shone above a shirt and tie, his white-blond hair slicked against his head. He had Joey on his arm. Jen thought it was one of the sweetest things she'd ever seen.

"I would call that your basic pity date," Caesar surmised, watching Joey and Andrew as they headed to the dance floor.

"Maybe Joey just likes Andrew," Jen mused.

"Right," Smelly scoffed. "No one likes the Bears."

"I do," Jen said. She turned to Walter, who loomed like the Hulk, the buttons on his shirt straining over his bulk. "Walter, may I have this dance?"

A slow smile, like sunshine, spread across Walter's round face. "We got it goin' on, pretty mama," he blustered. "Let's get down."

"Down where?" Jason asked, confused, just as a girl came over to him and shyly asked, "May I have this dance?"

"Yes!" Jason replied eagerly. "We get down, mama!"

Pacey watched his Bears from across the room. "Hey, maybe later on you'd like to dance with some of the guys from my bunk," he suggested to Tia.

"Oh no, you're my date," she insisted. "Besides, you're perfect."

"Trust me, Tia, I'm not even in the ballpark of perfect."

"But you are. You've taught me so much about acting this summer. You're so sensitive. And smart. And handsome. I wish the play wasn't tomorrow and that the summer was never going to end."

Pacey wasn't quite sure what to say. "I'm glad it's been a good experience for you, Tia."

She gazed up at him. "Will you call me when camp ends?"

"No," he said smiling, "but how about ten years from now?"

Tia looked crestfallen. "But I thought you liked me."

"I do like you! And if I were ten, I'd definitely call you. But I'm not."

"Well, when I'm twenty, you'll only be twenty-six, and it won't make any difference then," Tia said, "so I don't see why it should make so much difference now."

"It just does, sweetie," he told her gently. "I promise to stay your friend. How's that?" Her only answer was a sigh of regret.

The music changed to something fast. Jen and Walter kept dancing. "You're really good at this, Walter," Jen told him. "But, then, I already knew that from the play."

"I still can't believe I got the lead instead of Brad. I'm gonna be way nervous tomorrow night."

"You'll be great," Jen assured him.

"Yeah, but what if I—"

"Hi, Jen," Gigi called, dancing nearby with Pete. "Cute couple."

"Thanks," Jen said tersely.

"I know all about the little scam you and Charma the Androgynous are running," Gigi said. "I haven't decided what I intend to do about it yet. But don't assume you and Trevor have gotten away with this." Pete danced her off.

"What was that about, or is it none of my business?" Walter asked.

"Nothing important. Hey, I just noticed something, Walter."

"What's that?"

"You seem to have given up on the Ebonics."

Walter grinned. "Let's just say I be bilingual."

It was after midnight, and Trevor was fast asleep in the infirmary. He figured he'd have to spend the night there in order to make his illness believable. Staci was asleep in her room across the hall. He was the only "patient" there.

"Trevor?" a voice whispered in the dark. "Trevor?"

He opened his eyes and propped himself up on an elbow. "Who's there?"

"You know who."

High-heels in hand, Gigi tiptoed over to his bed. "Poor baby. So sick and all alone."

"And you've taken pity on me?" Trevor asked.

"Lucky you." She swung her shoes over his head.

He sat up. "I am a man of my word, lovely girl." He reached for her hand. "But you didn't have to threaten to turn Jen and me in for staying out past curfew to get me to spend the night with you, Gigi. All you had to do was ask."

"Talking is such a waste of time, Trevie. Wanna know what I feel like doing?"

"What?"

"Everything. Not to mince words, but are you 'up' for it?"

"Well now," Trevor began, "what if we go for the all-action, no-talk approach?"

She definitely agreed.

"Hold still!" Staci said as she cleaned the cut on Lillith's knee. The little girl's screams were way out of proportion to the extent of her very minor injury.

"I think she'll live," Staci assured Andie as the girl wiped tears from her cheeks.

"I need candy to make me feel better," Lillith insisted.

"Suck your thumb. It's more convenient," Staci suggested sweetly. "You can be the oldest thumb-sucker in the world."

Andie bit back a laugh. "Thanks for the emergency medical care," she told the nurse, who was putting a bandage on the girl's knee. "Well, we're off to the play-house to see *Grease*. You're coming, aren't you?"

"Sure," Staci replied. "I just need to straighten up the infirmary first. Trevor was sick last night and he slept in bed three. I need to change the sheets and remake the bed, but then I'll be down."

Andie took Lillith's hand. "Okay, see you there."

"Where's my candy?" Lillith demanded as Andie led her out the door.

Brat, Staci thought as she hustled to the linen closet to get fresh sheets for bed three. She smiled to herself. After the play, she had a date with Trevor, and she couldn't wait.

She brought fresh sheets into the infirmary and began to strip down the bed in which Trevor had slept. Laying there, between the sheets, was something pink and frilly. She gingerly picked it up: tiny bikini panties, with the name "Gigi" embroidered over the right hip.

Furious, Staci balled the panties up in her hand. Trevor had told her that Jen and Joey weren't wild enough for him, that the only one he really wanted was her. And she'd been dumb enough to believe him. She pitched Gigi's panties into the trash. Then she thought better of it and retrieved them.

Trevor was a dog. And he was going to pay.

From stage right, Jen and Pacey watched as the cast of *Grease* took their final bows to thunderous applause. Tia and Walter had been fabulous. Five minutes into the show, everyone had forgotten that they were only ten years old. The only person who had dropped a line was Brad. And Britney had sung her big solo in a completely different key than the one in which Trevor was accompanying her. Other than that, the show was a massive hit.

"Hey, standing O!" Pacey said, nudging Jen as the audience jumped to their feet.

"I gotta tell you, Pacey, I am really proud of them," Jen said, smiling.

"Yeah. Me too."

The cast ran offstage like they were supposed to, but the audience was still whooping and hollering. Walter and Tia looked up at Jen and Pacey for direction.

"Get back out there, you two!" Jen told them. "You deserve your own bow—sounds like your fans are demanding it."

Walter grabbed Tia's hand and they ran out onstage again, bowing as the cheers grew even louder.

"One performance," Pacey said, sighing, "after all that work. We really need to take this show on the road."

Jen laughed. "Trust me, Pacey. Everyone in the entire civilized world has already seen *Grease* multiple times. This isn't exactly Chekhov."

"Who's Chekhov?" Pacey asked. Jen shot him a look. "Kidding. I was kidding. Guess it's time to hit the cast party and get our accolades," he added.

"I have to meet Staci first."

"Staci, as in Nurse Staci?" Pacey asked. "What for?"

Jen shrugged. "Got me. She came running up to me right before curtain and said that it was crucial for me to meet her down at the dock right after the play. Life and death."

"Intriguing," Pacey mused. "Also bizarre. I will await your full report." He kissed her on the cheek. "It was great working with you on this, Jen."

"We were rather wonderful together," she agreed.

Jen went to each cast member and gave them a hug, assuring them she'd be at the cast party, before heading down to the waterfront.

There on the dock was Staci.

In Trevor's arms.

"Well, well," Jen said. "And what have we here? You must have run out after the play like a bat out of hell, Trevor, to beat me here."

"Jen!" Trevor gave her a cocky smile and took his hands off Staci. "Hey, wonderful job tonight, eh? The kids, I mean?"

"We'll get to the kids later," Jen said. "Staci invited me down here and I couldn't imagine why."

"And now you can," Staci filled in.

"Actually, no, I can't." Jen pushed some hair out of her eyes. "Did you think I'd hyperventilate because he's kissing you?"

"No," Staci replied, unperturbed.

"Hi," Joey said as she came up next to Jen. "Wait, I'm very confused. Staci, you left a message telling me I had to meet you down here after the play, so here I am." Her eyes went from Staci to Trevor to Jen. "So what's up?"

Staci smiled. "You will. Oh, look who else is coming down the path. Why, it's Gigi!"

For the first time, Trevor's cocky smile began to slip. "This is a regular convention, eh?"

"These are the kind of odds you like, isn't it, Trevor?" Staci asked innocently. "Hi, Gigi."

"Can we just bypass the chitchat?" Gigi asked. "I have serious PMS and I could swear there was dairy in the Tofutti I had for lunch because I'm all phlegmy. Now, what is the big emergency that you mentioned, Staci?"

"I thought we'd have a scavenger hunt," Staci said. "First person to come up with a pair of Gigi's panties wins." She reached into her pocket and brought out the pair she'd found in Trevor's bed. "I win!"

Gigi shook her red ponytail haughtily. "What did you do, steal those from my cabin?"

"Dream on," Staci said. She turned to Jen and Joey. "Love stud here wasn't sick last night. He asked me to cover for him and keep him in the infirmary and like an idiot I said yes. It seems he's been seeing both of you, and he told both of you he'd go to the dance with you last night."

Jen and Joey looked at each other. Then they looked at Trevor.

"It's not quite exactly how she makes it sound," he said lamely. "You could call it a . . . scheduling oversight"

"Imagine my surprise when I was making up the bed you slept in at the infirmary last night, Trevor, and found this stuffed between the sheets." She dangled Gigi's panties off one finger. "Wasn't it a little drafty, sneaking back into your cabin?"

Gigi's face turned bright red. "This is a setup. You stole those panties from me. It's my word against yours."

Jen cocked her head at Trevor. "So, as it turns out, you're rather juvenile and pathetic, huh?"

"I really do care for all of you," Trevor insisted. "You're all quite lovely and special."

Joey nodded. "You know, Trevor, you're right. I really can't speak for Gigi. But as for Staci and Jen and me, yes, we are quite singular and special. The problem is, you aren't."

In a moment of perfect female mind-meld, Staci, Jen, and Joey marched right up to Gigi and Trevor. And pushed both of them off the dock. Trevor and Gigi screamed and thrashed around in the water.

"You'll pay for this!" Gigi screamed.

"I have this wonderfully self-satisfied feeling," Jen said. "Don't you?" Staci and Joey nodded their agreement. "My only regret, Staci, is that Joey and I didn't get to know you earlier in the summer. What say the three of us hit the cast party and make up for lost time?"

Chapter 13

"Having fun?" Joey asked Dawson, as she sidled over to him and Pacey.

"In an oddly Americana sort of way," Dawson admitted. "Who invented color war anyway?"

"Ancient Aztecs," Pacey deadpanned. "Part of their fertility rites."

At that moment, Trevor walked by with Gigi. They both pretended that Joey didn't even exist. Dawson gave Joey a quizzical look. "You don't mind sharing your current flame with the camp tramp?"

"As much as I detest Gigi—and we're talking mucho detest—I would appreciate it if you did not ever refer to any girl as—and I quote—a 'tramp.'"

Pacey's fist pumped the air. "Get down with that sisterhood is powerful rap, my sistuh."

"Not funny," Joey told him. "To continue, Dawson.

Trevor is not my current anything. I think he and Gigi make a lovely couple." She smiled at him sweetly. "Catch you later. My bunk awaits their color war orders for the afternoon."

Dawson scratched his head. "Did that make even a modicum of sense to you, Pacey?"

"Nope," Pacey said cheerfully. "And just to add to your confusion, when I asked Jen this morning if she was going to see Mr. Tall, Buff, and English after camp ended, she said, 'Are you on drugs?' "

Dawson shrugged. "Forget it. Women are incomprehensible. He took in the immense crowd that had gathered around the Boys versus Girls Color War scoreboard, which had been erected on the beach outside the dining hall. As Mr. Tacky had hoped, the battle of the sexes had attracted a tremendous amount of camper enthusiasm, not to mention distracting the campers from the fact that their session would soon be over and they would be going home.

The scoreboard broke down color war by events. Girl teams had competed against boy teams in all of them, by age groups. A win gave your team ten points, a loss gave your team zero points. Dawson cupped his hand to his brow to block out the afternoon sun and read the scores listed thus far.

	Takabec Boys	Takabec Girls
BASEBALL		
Ages 7 and 8	10	0
Ages 8 and 9	10	0
Ages 10–12	10	0
Ages 13–14	0	10

	Takabec Boys	Takabec Girls
SAILBOAT RACING		
Ages 7–10	0	10
Ages 11–14	10	0
SKIT COMPETITION	0	10

It went on and on; they were coming to the end of two solid days of competition. And amazingly, the score was tied at two hundred points per team, with only one event left. Mr. Tacky called it the famous Wacked-Up Relay Race.

"The Wacked-Up Relay was a Camp Homeric tradition," he'd told them all at lunch, "and we're going to continue it here. It allows all campers to participate; in fact, every camper must participate. Each team will have a runner, and that runner will run from event to event and cannot go on to the next event until the camper participating in that event has successfully completed his mission."

"I sincerely hope we're not being tested on this," Pacey had told Dawson. "Because I have zero idea what the man just said. How about you?"

"Clueless."

But Mr. Tack went on enthusiastically. "For example, the first event is the bed-making competition, between the seven-year-old boys and seven-year-old girls. We'll assemble beds on the boys' quad. The runners will begin at the nature lodge and run to the boys' quad. Then, the seven-year-olds will strip the beds down to their mattresses and remake them. My nephew, Pete, will be the judge of when the beds have been made neatly. When he gives the okay, the runners will go on to their next event. And you're in luck, Andie McPhee," he added, "no need for plastic sheeting!"

Andie's young girls shrunk with embarrassment. "What a moron," Andie said under her breath as the older campers laughed with delight. Once the Tackmeister got over his own mirth, he went on.

"So," Mr. Tack continued, "we'll assemble at the beach at two o'clock, everyone will go to their assignments, and we'll start the relay at three. The whole thing should take two hours, and may the best team win! Counselors, pick up your bunk's Wacked-Up Relay assignment in my office after lunch. Remember, good sportsmanship is our motto here at Camp Takabec," he added, then grinned mischievously, "but what really counts is winning!"

"Mr. Tack rules! Mr. Tack rules!" some boys began to chant. The camp director waved at them.

"Notice how he's got that Miss America thing going on with his wrist as he waves," Pacey noted.

"Yeah, I had him pegged as a closet case from the beginning," Jack deadpanned. "Catch you guys later." He walked off.

"So, what torture has the Tacky One come up with for our kids?" Pacey asked Dawson, since Dawson had gone to the office to pick up the bunk's assignment.

Dawson looked down at the sheet of paper in his hand. "Meeting on the basketball court, doing Dizzy Dribbling. What's Dizzy Dribbling?"

An older boy who had overheard what Dawson

said laughed. "Dizzy Dribbling? Man, Tack *really* hates you guys. It's the last event of the Wacked-Up Relay. Your guys dribble the basketball down the court, at the end they get spun around and around by a counselor, and then they have to dribble back to where they started without falling over. Most kids barf about two seconds into it."

"Swell," Pacey said.

"But that's ludicrous!" Dawson objected. "How can an adult invent an activity that he knows will make kids sick?"

"Not to worry," the older kid said as he walked off, "they always have a nurse on hand. Bandages. Buckets. Whatever."

Pacey and Dawson exchanged looks. "I am more glad than ever that our guys have planned such a fitting surprise for that bilious pile of protoplasm passing himself off as a camp director," Dawson said with disgust.

"I'm with you, my friend," Pacey agreed. "Well, let's go break the sad news to our bunk."

Pacey and Dawson headed up the hill to the boys' quad. "What really irritates the hell out of me is that Tack gave our guys Dizzy Dribbling so that he can humiliate them one last time," Dawson fumed. "And don't tell we're going to get back at him with the secret project. That won't stop the rest of the camp from laughing at the Bears in the meantime."

"Life sucks, then you die," Pacey philosophized.

The Bears, except for Andrew, were gathered around Kenny's bed, looking at something or other. Andrew was alone, typing into his laptop.

"Lemme see!" Alan hooted from somewhere in the mass of boys. "Wow, did you get a look at those ta-tas? You think they're real?"

"I'd have to feel to know for sure," Smelly smirked.

Dawson tapped Smelly on his back. "Hi, there."

The Bears whirled to look at Dawson, utterly guilty looks on their faces, as Kenny threw something under his bed.

"Chill," Pacey told them. "I ogled many a girl with a staple in her navel in my young and innocent years."

"We'll go with the 'Don't ask, don't tell policy,'" Dawson instantly decided. "So we're going to pretend we never saw whatever it was that we just didn't see. Okay, we've got your assignment for the final color war event."

"What is it?" Smelly asked, relief in his voice. "No, wait. Don't tell me, it's Dizzy Dribbling."

"What be Dizzy Dribblin'?" Jason asked.

Smelly laid it out for all his bunkmates. "Last summer at Homeric," he went on, "one kid who did Dizzy Dribbling barfed up his own esophagus."

"Look, you guys just go out there and do the best you can," Pacey told them. "Dawson and I will be with you all the way. Right, Dawson?"

"Right," Dawson agreed.

"Yeah?" Alan asked. "I don't see you volunteering to do it."

"Campers only," Pacey reminded him. "Them's the rules."

"Well, the rules be suckin'," Walter groused. "And

all the props I been getting 'cuz I be so good in the play gonna be all forgotten, 'cuz everyone gonna be laughin' at me."

Pacey regarded him thoughtfully. "I never knew it was possible to create a sentence with so many grammatical mistakes."

Andrew looked even whiter than usual. "Do you think it might be possible to get a medical dispensation from this activity?"

Suddenly, Caesar bounced up on his bed. "Medical dispensation?" he asked rhetorically. "That's it. I've got it!"

"What you got?" Jason asked.

"I know how we can kick butt Dizzy Dribbling!"

He ran to his cubbyhole, grabbed a large paper sack that was on the bottom, and pawed through it, throwing various medications over his shoulder as he scrounged around. "Got it!" He held up a small white package.

"What be that?" Jason asked.

Caesar was too busy cracking up to answer Jason's question. No one else had the slightest clue as to what was going on. Caesar waved them over. "Come here, guys. I'll tell you the plan. And when I'm done, you're all gonna be calling me a genius."

"Go, Kendall! Go!" the girls lining the route to the basketball cheered for Kendall, who had been selected as the runner for the girls' team. "We're winning, so go, go!" An impromptu group of cheerleaders, directed by Gigi, was leading the cheering.

Meanwhile, back down at the waterfront, Charma

was delaying the boys' runner, the burly Roger Repoz, from starting toward the final event, because the thirteen-year-old boys in the war canoe event had tried to cheat by skipping one of the marker buoys. But Charma had been watching the whole race with her binoculars, and when the race was over she assessed a three-minute penalty. The boys had been up in arms because the penalty had put them behind in the Wacked-Up Relay. But the penalty stood.

"Go!" Charma yelled, giving Roger the signal that he could move on. The boys lining the road cheered as Roger tore up toward the basketball court. They knew that the Bears had been selected for Dizzy Dribbling and every second was crucial. The reputation of the Bears as a bunch of geeky klutzes hadn't changed a bit. As Roger passed them on the road, the boys fell in behind him, racing toward the basketball court.

Meanwhile, up the court, the Bears stood assembled at one end near the sideline, and a bunk of ten-year-old girls was at the other. In between stood Mr. Takermann himself. The stands were jammed with campers of both sexes.

"Remember," Mr. Takermann warned both groups. "You can't go until I blow the whistle. Girls, you run to Jen at the far end. Jen, spin each girl ten times. No cheating. Guys, you run to Jack. Ten times, Jack. Dribble up, dribble down, and—whoa, I see Kendall coming now!"

The girls in the stands cheered as Kendall came into view, running at full tilt. She ran to the basketball goal and banged it with her relay baton.

Tweet! "Girls, go!" the Tack called. The first girl started dribbling down the court toward Jen as the boys in the stands booed lustily. As for the Bears, they stood around, knowing that the crowd was anticipating yet another moment of their humiliation.

Four girls had completed the up-and-back by the time Roger came barreling toward the basketball court. The "up" had been easy, but after they'd been spun by Jen and thoroughly dizzied, the "back" had been deadly treacherous—all the girls had fallen down. In any case, the boys were way, way behind when Roger banged his baton on the basketball goal post.

Tweet! "Go boys!" Mr. Takermann yelled. Caesar was the first dribbler. He dribbled the ball easily down the court to Jack, then allowed himself to be spun around ten times. Time for the return trip, where he'd be going crazily all over the place because he was so dizzy.

But it didn't happen. He dribbled back to the Bears' end as easily as he'd done the first part of his dribbling and handed the ball off to Smelly.

"Go, Smelly!" he shouted as the boys in the crowd cheered crazily and Mr. Takermann stared at him in abject shock. Smelly dribbled up and back with nary a bob or weave. The same thing happened with Kenny. Walter. Jason. They dribbled the length of the court easily, in both directions, as if Jack's spinning had no effect on them at all.

"How cool is this?" Pacey screamed at Dawson so he could be heard over the wildly cheering crowd.

"Extremely!" Dawson called back.

The Bears had nearly caught up now. Andrew was the last dribbler. He took the ball from Alan and carefully started dribbling down the court toward Jack, just as the last girl was being spun around by Jen.

"Casper! Casper! Casper!" the Bears chanted.

"Bears, Bears, Bears!" the other boys in the stands were chanting. It was bedlam. Jen released the last girl, who started dribbling back toward the end line, stumbling around as if she were drunk. All the other girls screamed at her to keep going, no matter what. Andrew reached Jack, who whirled him ten times quickly. Then, he turned toward home. He dribbled as fast as his diminutive body would carry him.

"Bears, Bears, Bears!" the shouting continued.

Andrew and the last girl crossed the line in a dead heat, and everyone went wild. The boys, who had given up all hope of winning, poured out of the stands, rushed to the Bears, and hoisted them onto their shoulders, shouting and pummeling them with joyous high-fives.

"You realize that I would never write a third-act love fest that is this cliché-ridden," Dawson told Pacey.

Pacey smiled. "Yeah. I know."

The celebration continued as Mr. Tack engaged in a hurried conference with his nephew. Finally, he blew his whistle for attention. It took three blasts to get the campers to calm down. Mr. T climbed up on the basketball bleachers to address the crowd.

"Campers of Camp Takabec," he shouted, "you have witnessed a remarkable event this afternoon.

Never before has the Wacked-Up Relay ended in a tie. But there must be a winner, and there will be a tiebreaker. My assistant and I have determined that we will break the tie by a football throw-and-catch competition to be held immediately at the football field. Let's get going!" He stabbed the air in the direction of the football field.

Like a human wave, the campers all ran toward the football field.

"Yo, Dawson," Jen called, catching up with him, "how did your bunk manage to dribble like that?"

Dawson reached into his pocket and held up an empty package. "Caesar, our bunk hypochondriac, gave 'em all Dramamine for motion sickness. It stabilizes your sense of balance. Evidently it worked."

Jen laughed. "That kid is a hoot. Your Bears are now enjoying their fifteen minutes of fame. And it's well deserved."

Once everyone was assembled at the football field, Mr. Tack explained what the tiebreaker would be. The boys would choose one athlete, the girls would choose one as well. Those two athletes would each have a shot at trying to catch a long pass thrown by Mr. Tack himself. First, the girl would play defense. Then, they'd switch roles, and the girl would catch a pass thrown by Jack. Whoever caught the longer pass would win the color war for their team.

"Well, I strenuously object to this plan," Andie told her friends. "Mr. Tack will make sure he throws a great pass to the guy. And on top of that, everyone knows that girls lack the upper-body strength to be really good at football."

"It doesn't take upper-body strength to catch a pass, Andie," her brother said. Dawson's eyes met Jack's. He had a feeling he knew exactly what Jack was planning. The girl campers, however, had no idea. And so they groaned and protested when Mr. T made his announcement.

"Excuse me, Mr. T!" Gigi called, waving her hand in the air. "But I really feel that in the spirit of fairness, we should at least also have a cheerleading competition to even things out." No one paid the least attention to her.

The boys named Roger Repoz as their athlete. Jack huddled with the girls. This was a no-brainer. Even if they were going to get their butts kicked at this final event, they had to give it their best shot, which meant they'd use the only girl at camp who was on the football team: Cassie.

"That is, unless you want to do it, Gigi," Jack added innocently.

"Oh, very funny," she snapped.

Roger got ready to receive the first pass from Mr. Tack, with Cassie defending. Jack blew a whistle to start the competition, and the crowd went wild as Roger ran right at Cassie. He outweighed her by at least forty pounds and was a lot taller. But Cassie stayed right with him. Mr. Tack let fly with his pass. It was slightly underthrown, and Cassie knocked it away.

The girls went wild with joy, and the boys all booed. Cassie trotted back to Jack, and Roger followed, glowering with anger.

"That was a bogus pass, man!" Roger yelled at the camp director.

Jack put an arm around Cassie. "You ready?" She nodded.

"Good." Jack kept his voice low. "He'll be thinking short, Cassie. Twenty-five slant, on two. Go!"

Cassie assumed a two-point stance as Roger lined up across from her. Mr. Tack blew his whistle, and Cassie ran three yards and whirled. Roger, knowing that only a short pass had to be completed, committed himself to defend.

That was when Cassie spun completely around and slipped past Roger, heading for the far goal line. Jack's pass was perfect, and Cassie made an over-the-shoulder catch. She kept running toward the end zone as the girls, this time, went insane with happiness.

"Girls win!" Jen cried, and Joey and Andie took up the chant with them. "Girls win, girls win, girls win!" The cheering went on for fifteen minutes. Color war was over. The Bears had won their dignity, but the girls had won the war.

Chapter 14

"And so it is with great pride, as well as a tear in my eye, that I most humbly thank all of you for helping to make the first month of Camp Takabec the phenomenal success that it was," Mr. Tack told the assembled throng of campers and staff.

The camp director stood underneath a huge banner that read Camp Takabec Final Banquet, made by Jocy and volunteer campers in arts and crafts. Resting on the podium were several small trophies, a larger trophy for the winners of color war that would stay in his office and be engraved with the words Girls 2000, and a single gigantic trophy that would go to the bunk named Best Bunk of the Twenty-first Century.

Mr. Tack had been using the Best Bunk award as leverage to improve campers' behavior. Camp oddsmakers were calling it the Lions, five to one.

The entire staff and all the campers were assembled in the dining hall. They'd just finished a dinner that actually bordered on edible. For dessert, a giant sheet cake had been wheeled out of the kitchen to great applause. Walter was wearing some of the frosting on his T-shirt.

Each bunk was flying a flag they'd created that represented the uniqueness of their bunk. Since none of the Bears had any artistic talent whatsoever, and none of them had any interest in making the stupid flag in the first place, theirs was simply a piece of felt with big cut-out lettering that read The Bears, which, Dawson figured, probably let them out of being in contention for best flag.

As Mr. Tack stopped to take a sip of water, Pacey leaned close to Dawson. "You really think this is gonna work?"

"It's worth a shot."

"Unless it backfires and the Tackmeister decides to blacken our employment records from here to eternity," Pacey added. "Not that such a thing would disturb me, since I'm considering a career as a professional sloth. You, however, Dawson, were meant for bigger and better things."

"A risk I'm willing to take," Dawson replied.

"And now, the moment you've all been waiting for," the camp director continued, "our awards ceremony. We begin with the trophy for Best Bunk flag. The winner is . . . the Pussycats!"

The nine-year-old girls jumped up and down at their table, hugging one another. Their flag featured three-dimensional kittens with moving paws and long false eyelashes. The girls and their counselors got up to receive their trophy.

On and on the trophy ceremony went. Best Bunk Spirit. Best Bunk Athletes, Best Cheer, Best Skit, etcetera. The Bears got so bored that they began to draw tattoos on one another with permanent ink pens.

After that, Mr. Tack moved on to the individual awards. Best Female Athlete: Cassie Myers. Jack punched his fist into the air, he was so happy for her. And all the girls in the camp cheered her name as she went up for her trophy. After all, she had won color war for them. Britney won most talented, which many of the other campers booed.

When the individual trophy winners had all been announced, Mr. Tack presented the color war trophy to the girls. "That was quite a color war upset, ladies," he told the crowd. "But I have a feeling the guys are gonna get back at you next summer!" His words kicked off minutes of over-the-top cheering and chanting from the boys, except for the Bears.

Mr. Tack motioned with his hands for the guys to settle down, and they finally did. "I know everyone is anxious to find out which bunk has been named Best Bunk, and I'm gosh-darned excited about it, myself."

He fingered the giant, gleaming trophy, which stood at least three feet high. "If I might be serious for a moment, kids," he went on. "Camping should bring out the best in you. Camping should teach you to be first-rate and to take pride in yourself and your accomplishments. I know the members of the winning bunk, as well as their counselors, exemplify all that is the best and brightest of Camp Takabec. I'd be proud to call each and every one of them my own sons or daughters."

The campers applauded and cheered.

"Before I award this final, and most meaningful, of trophies," the camp director said, "the film club, led by Dawson Leery, has a special treat for us. It's a film they made over the past four weeks that is the story of us all, Camp Takabec, the shining, glorious, inspirational story of you. Dawson?"

Dawson and the kids who had worked on the film—there were a dozen of them, of all different ages—came forward, and Pacey adjusted a screen in front of the podium. Someone in the back turned out the lights, and the documentary began.

A stark black screen lit up with the title: Camp Takabec: The Best Summer Ever!

The film began. It was full of candid moments over the past month that the film club had managed to capture—the bonfire, swimming, football games, the camp play, it went on and on. Kids laughed when they saw themselves or their friends doing funny things. Everyone was totally absorbed in the film.

Mr. Takermann had moved to the back of the dining hall, the better to watch the documentary. Dawson tapped him on the shoulder.

"Might I have a word with you, sir?" Dawson asked, his voice low.

"Not now, Dawson. I'm watching your film. I have to tell you, you did a bang-up job."

"Thank you. The matter at hand can't wait, Mr.

Takermann. I would have to say it's something of an emergency."

Clearly irritated, the camp director followed Dawson into the kitchen. Waiting for him was Pacey and the Bears.

"For pity's sake, what is going on here?" Mr. Tack asked irritably. "Is someone ill?"

"It's critical that you see this, sir," Pacey said.

"See *what?*"

Pacey nodded toward a portable TV/VCR combo that had been set up on the stainless steel counter. Pacey pressed the On button.

On the black screen: Camp Takabec: The Summer from Hell.

"The guys named it themselves," Pacey added fondly. "They've already made multiple copies—you know how parents love those souvenirs of their kids at camp—but they thought you might like to see it first."

"What is this?" Mr. Tack blustered, but his eyes were riveted to the screen. The movie began with a close-up of the camp director, his face mottled with fury. The camera pulled back to show him screaming at the Bears, calling them losers, weenies, a disgrace to his camp. Following that, there were various moments when Mr. Tack had berated the Bears individually—calling Walter a "fat disgrace," withholding Andrew's inhaler, and kicking dirt at Caeser when he struck out at baseball.

From there, it cut to Mr. Tack in his private office, beer in one hand, cigarette in the other, with Gigi sitting on his lap, giggling.

"How dare you?" the camp director sputtered. "Where—how—did you get that?"

"I be tricky," Jason said proudly. "Film from window."

The tape went from bad to worse, and ended with more compromising activity in Mr. Tack's office.

"Correct me if I'm wrong, Mr. Tack," Pacey began, "but I seem to recall that you're married, right? And your wife is in Europe, didn't you tell us? Don't think the little lady's gonna be too pleased with this memorabilia."

"Turn it off," Mr. Tack commanded.

"But there's so much more," Dawson told him. "And the Bears worked so hard on it."

"I *said* turn it off!"

"Well, when you put it like that." Pacey pushed the Off button on the VCR.

"Let's cut to the chase, shall we?" the camp director snapped. "What the hell is it you people want? Money? Are you blackmailing me, you slimy little bastards?"

Walter sauntered over to the camp director and got right in his face. "We don't be needing your damn money, fool."

Mr. Tack shrunk away from him. "What, then?"

"How about if you begin with an apology?" Andrew suggested. "To everyone, that is."

"We know you won't mean it," Kenny added, "but we don't care. We saved our rep yesterday at Dizzy Dribbling, but we want them to hear from you."

"A public apology," the camp director repeated stiffly. "Is that it?"

"Two things more," Jason told him.

Walter folded his arms cockily. "It's like this. We wanna come back to camp next summer. And we wanna all be together, one bunk."

"Fine, fine, you deserve each other," Mr. Tack said.

"But it's going to be a different kind of camp, Mr. Tack," Caesar said. "Because if you so much as humiliate one kid, ever again, we'll send copies of this tape to every parent."

Mr. Tack turned to Dawson and Pacey. "You're letting them get away with this?"

"You shouldn't have messed with the Bears," Pacey told him.

Mr. Tack's hands clenched into fists. "*Fine*. What else?"

Andrew stepped forward. "Last, but hardly least, sir. You are about to name us Best Bunk."

"But . . . but that's heresy!"

"You no be calling shunts," Jason told him.

"That's 'shots,'" Andrew corrected. "And Mr. Tack, you'd better give a really great speech telling everyone how wonderful we are before you present us with that trophy. Any questions?"

"None," the camp director barked.

"I'd suggest you get your butt out there, sir," Pacey told him. "The film club's documentary of Camp Takabec is about to end."

"And we've got a copy of this video all set to go," Dawson added.

"You boys are loathsome," Mr. Takermann spat.

"Nah. We rule," Walter said with a grin. "And you gonna go tell everyone exactly that. Deal?"

The camp director struggled, but clearly he could think of no alternative. "Deal," he finally said.

"And now, campers, the big moment," Mr. Tack said. His words were warm but his eyes were cold. At the Bears' table, everyone held their breath.

"The winners of Best Bunk, the group that embodies all the finest qualities of Camp Takabec, is . . . the Bears."

The Bears jumped out of their seats, cheering at the top of their lungs, as they ran forward to claim their trophy. Most of the other campers were in a state of shock.

"But they're weenies! They suck!" one of the Lions yelled.

Caesar shot Mr. Tack a warning look.

"No, they don't," the camp director said stiffly. "They showed true camp spirit when they came through in Dizzy Dribbling. They are fine young men. And furthermore, I don't tolerate that kind of language at this camp."

Walter grabbed the giant trophy and hoisted it over his head as the campers, with some notable exceptions, now cheered for the Bears.

"Good work, my friend," Pacey told Dawson, smiling at their ecstatic campers. He fist-bumped Dawson. "I don't know about you, but I'm getting a Kodak commercial warm-fuzzy kind of feeling."

Dawson's eyes shone. "The only difference, Pace, is that our kids are real. And they're great."

"Jack! Jack!"

Jack turned around. Amid the teeming crowds of

campers and parents and relatives who had come to pick them up, he picked out Cassie, running toward him.

"I'm so glad I found you," Cassie said breathlessly. "I wanted to have a chance to say goodbye. And to thank you for everything you did for me."

Jack gave her a warm hug. "It was more than my pleasure, Cassie. You're a terrific kid."

"I just want you to remember, I won't be a kid forever, Jack McPhee. Who knows? Six years from now, I might just look you up."

"You are one remarkable twelve-year-old."

"I'm almost thirteen," she said significantly. Then she stood on tiptoe to kiss his cheek and ran off into the crowd.

"Hey, Jack," Andie said, hurrying over to him. "I saw Cassie kiss you goodbye just now. That was so sweet."

Jack smiled wistfully. "Almost makes me wish that six years from now, if she looks me up, I'd be the kind of guy who could appreciate it. You see your brood off?"

"All the parents have picked up their little darlings. Lillith introduced Toni and Maya to her parents as her African friends. She got confused."

"Did you intervene in your usual gracious manner?"

"Yes, as a matter of fact," Andie told him. "I was an exemplary counselor, if I do say so myself."

"Did it bring out your maternal instincts?"

Andie made a face. "God, no. I'm just an obsessive perfectionist, you know that."

Jack draped an arm around his sister's shoulders. "Yeah, sis. I do."

Not far away, Andrew's parents shook Pacey's hand, then Dawson's, and looked proudly at their son.

"Andrew told us this was the best summer he's ever had in his life," Mrs. Casparian told them. "He thinks the world of the two of you."

"We feel the same way about him," Dawson told her.

"It's funny, really," Mr. Casparian mused, "because the first few letters he sent home were full of pleadings for us to let him come home. I guess things turned around for you, huh, son?" He playfully pulled down the brim of Andrew's omnipresent baseball cap.

"You could say that," Andrew agreed.

"Yo, Casper!" Walter called, running over to them as fast as his bulk allowed. The rest of the Bears were right behind him.

"Hi, you guys," Andrew said.

"What did they call you, honey?" his mother asked.

"Casper. I like it." He introduced the Bears to his parents. "We're gonna be a bunk together next summer too," he told his parents.

"Bet we be Best Bunk next summer too," Jason said slyly. He fingered a copy of their secret video that was sticking out of a mammoth pocket on his baggy jeans.

"Will you boys be counselors here next summer?" Mr. Casparian asked Dawson and Pacey. "I know it would mean a lot to Andrew."

"To all of us," Walter added.

"Thanks for the vote of confidence," Dawson said. "We'll definitely consider it."

They said a final goodbye to all the Bears and headed for the office to get their final paychecks for the summer.

"Would you really consider coming back here next summer to be a counselor?" Dawson asked Pacey. "The summer before we start college?"

"About as much chance as the Tackmeister finding God and joining a monastery," Pacey replied. "Whoa, check that out." He pointed to the camp arch, where Gigi and Trevor were in the midst of an impassioned conversation. Dawson and Pacey watched as Gigi slapped Trevor across the face, before stomping away.

"And here I thought they made the perfect couple," Pacey said. "Where's the love?"

"Hey, you guys about ready to blow this pop stand?" Jen asked, catching up with them.

"We just need to pick up our checks," Dawson told her. "Did you happen to witness the soap-opera moment between Gigi and Trevor just now?"

"Sure did. Can't say that I blame her," Jen replied.

"Why?" Dawson asked. "I am utterly confused."

"Gigi read Trevor's mail this morning. Turns out he's got a fiancée back in England."

"Unbelievable," Dawson marveled.

"I am so on the cusp of admiring the guy, I can't tell you," Pacey admitted.

"Does Joey know about this too?" Dawson asked.

Jen nodded. "And so does Staci. He was playing all of us."

"What a cad," Pacey said dramatically. "Toying with the affections of innocent, young girls—"

"What affections?" Jen asked.

Dawson gave her a look. "You mean, you're not upset?"

"Why would I be upset?"

Before Dawson could formulate an answer, Joey called to them from steps of the playhouse. "Hey, let's get this show on the road! We're outta here."

"Kindly enlighten me, Joey," Dawson said when they reached the step. "Jen filled us in on the extent of Trevor's perfidy. She isn't at all upset. Are you?"

"Of course not," said Joey.

Dawson shook his head. "How can that possibly make sense?"

Jen sighed with exasperation. "Read my lips, Dawson. Trevor. Was. Just. For. Fun."

"How shallow," Pacey chided.

Jen shrugged. "Sorry we aren't the tender flowers you two imagined. Now excuse us, we're going to pick up our very well-deserved paychecks." She and Joey headed into the playhouse, where Mr. Takermann had set up his office for the day.

"It's almost like they're on a different planet from us," Pacey mused.

"Planet Inconsistent," Dawson said. "They complain bitterly about guys using girls, then they write off Trevor's antics as inconsequential."

"You realize what this means, Dawson. We may have to spend the next sixty, seventy years of our lives trying to figure them out."

Dawson thought about that for a moment. "I can deal with that."

They picked up their checks, deliberately skipping a protracted goodbye scene with the camp director. A half-hour later, Dawson, Pacey, Jack, Joey, Jen, and Andie were assembled at the camp arch, bags at their side, ready to go.

"It was quite an experience," Andie said. "Not one that I'm anxious to repeat, however."

"The question is, what are we going to do for the rest of the summer?" Dawson asked.

"Do you ever stop planning?" Pacey asked him. "How about if we just wallow in hormonally driven decadence? The prison known as high school is right around the corner, you know." They picked up their gear and headed for Pacey's truck.

"We could go rock climbing," Andie suggested. "Or scuba. They're giving lessons at the Y."

They all began talking at once, arguing about what they should do with their remaining few weeks of freedom. Dawson looked over at Joey. "Ever wish the summer would never end, Joe?"

"All the time, Dawson. But it always does."

"Hey, how about if we rent *St. Elmo's Fire* tonight?" Andie suggested. "It reminds me so much of us."

Pacey, Jack, and Jen began arguing with her, and Dawson caught Joey's eye again. Then he reached out and took her hand. Summer would end. Dawson knew that.

But the important thing was, the six of them would not.

About the Author

C. J. Anders is a pseudonym for a well-known young adult fiction–writing couple.

A selected list of Dawson's Creek books available from Channel 4 Books

The prices shown below are correct at time of going to press. However, Channel 4 Books reserve the right to show new retail prices on covers which may differ from those previously advertised.

The Beginning of Everything Else	Jennifer Baker	£3.99
Long Hot Summer	K. S. Rodriguez	£3.99
Shifting Into Overdrive	C. J. Anders	£3.99
Major Meltdown	K. S. Rodriguez	£3.99
Double Exposure	C. J. Anders	£3.99
Trouble in Paradise	C. J. Anders	£3.99
Calm Before the Storm	Jennifer Baker	£3.99
Don't Scream	C. J. Anders	£3.99
Too Hot To Handle	C. J. Anders	£3.99
Tough Enough	C. J. Anders	£3.99
Playing for Keeps	C. J. Anders	£3.99
Dawson's Creek Omnibus I	Baker/Rodriguez/Anders	£5.99
Dawson's Creek Omnibus II	Rodriguez/Anders/Baker	£5.99
Dawson's Creek Official Postcard Book		£4.99

All Dawson's Creek titles can be ordered from your local bookshop or simply by ringing our 24 hour hotline on 01624 844444, email *bookshop@enterprise.net*, fax 01624 837033 or fill in this form and post it to Bookpost PLC, PO Box 29, Douglas, Isle of Man IM99 1BQ.
Please make all cheques payable to Channel 4 Books.

Name ————————————————————————————

Address ——————————————————————————

————————————————————————————————

————————————————————————————————

Card Name: Visa ❏ American Express ❏ Mastercard ❏ Switch ❏ please tick one

Expiry date ————/————/————

POSTAGE AND PACKAGING FREE FOR ALL ADDRESSES IN THE UK

www.panmacmillan.com   www.channel4.com